Advanc
A Gathering

MW00326199

". . . an ambitious, varied collection with a number of standout stories. . . Shaw shows flashes of brilliance and is able to move readers. . . This meticulous volume is a courageous attempt to reflect the multifaceted nature of New York life, and the final offering, which portrays the empty metropolis as 'drained of its blood,' is both timely and chilling. . . intelligently conceived."

Kirkus Reviews

"The stories are so striking; I can taste the meals described and hear the characters speaking. They are intense! The memories jump off the page! I've lived in the Big Apple and written about it for so many years, yet these stories paint vivid images of the city that are new to me. Particularly for me, the stories of the yin and yang of the Chinese immigrant experience in New York ring personal and true. The craftsmanship is superior."

Rebecca Liew,
short story author and poet,
World Journal

"Shaw paints a lively series of New York City character portraits over a 60-year timespan, each from an entirely different point of view . . . Shaw's portraits are overwhelmingly sympathetic, no matter his subjects' sins or crimes, though he also never sugarcoats them . . . The tales all share a pattern of storytelling cadence despite their frequently disparate subject matter as Shaw celebrates the rhythms of the city itself—and those who find ways to survive in it."

BookLife

A GATHERING OF BROKEN MIRRORS

MEMORIES OF SURVIVORS IN NEW YORK

ANTHONY E. SHAW

atmosphere press

ALSO BY
ANTHONY E. SHAW

CONTENTS

Dedicated to my brother Joseph McCourt
and the memory of Irena Sendler,
who chose God and life.

PREFACE

Our daily lives are a precarious dance between now and death.

Being created means being destroyed. A force of good exists with an opposing force of evil. To be joyous requires we know how to grieve. To live means we must die. From birth, we engage in the finite competition for existence and survival. This existence has two faces, and they are the ultimate challenge that we are front and center with every single day on the marathon dance floor that is life's stage.

How do we whirl in the middle of a busy, crowded space and survive?

If we were all angels, this would be heaven and we would fly, but we aren't, this isn't, and we don't. There are curves and bumps along the way. Detours leading to stone walls. Exits that bring us back to step one. Often the directions change or are unknown. We each take different steps, dancing at different speeds, and there are no bleachers for us to take a time-out. We stumble and fall and try to pick ourselves up to keep going. We are bruised and blessed, lost and found; we fail and succeed, are kindly and monstrous. Fruitful and destructive. Vulnerable and protected. We can spin so swiftly, we lose sight of where we might stop.

Nothing is perfect because we are imperfect.

Against all these obstacles, we keep dancing.

Every day, God and the prince of this world are side by

side on the streets of the city. We share the sidewalks and the gutters, the alleys and the avenues, the homes, shelters, offices, stores, bus stops, subway stations, attics, closets, and basements with them. They forgive and punish us, moment by moment, offering salvation and damnation at the same time. Death is an active double agent, working for either one or both.

Our lives revolve around their presence, unseen for the most part, unless we deliberately take the time to stop, look, and feel to find our way. Clear-sighted or blind, we weigh our progress in life and take our steps.

We are never alone in sunshine and darkness; the marathon goes on.

We fall asleep on our feet, in the hope we will either wake up or that someone or something will prop us up until we resume.

We move about and convince ourselves that when our freedom is limited by the order around us, that is our life's boundary – but it isn't. To survive, we embrace the unknown, the unwelcome, and the uncertain, because they are there waiting for us outside the borders, whether we understand them or like them or are able to meet them full square. We attempt to redefine good and evil, and we fail miserably every time.

Our blessing can be a disaster, and our curse can be a healing.

This is the dance of life, the next steps of which are always different or the last.

We are all sinners. We perish. We go to the next place.

The following voices talk about survivors traveling to the end.

Each story is a solitary one about a different person, in

a different time and setting. A number of them go back to childhood; some speak in their present. Though none of them is me, they are all in me – I am their witness. They ask the questions that I still ask.

Forty years ago, I visited my older brother, a professor of law and provost at Ohio State University, in Columbus. He hadn't set foot in our home in Brooklyn in more than fifteen years. When I asked him how it felt to be an Ohioan, he replied testily, "I'm a New Yorker," intentionally divorcing himself spiritually from his transplanted physical environs. New York is not a place; it's a mood, an emotion, an opinion. It defies sense and confounds logic. New York is not stationary. It was, it is, and it will be, simultaneously. It cannot be defined in mere static words, but only in stories that are the scattered emotional pieces of lives lived. It is a mirror – look into it and see life's images looking back, often broken and missing fragments.

Those images are life lived as memories, and according to Tennessee Williams, "Memory is seated predominantly in the heart." A heart that doesn't stand still, but continues to beat and feel. Dr. Alfred Adler called memory one of life's most revealing psychic expressions: an intentionally chosen reminder. The artist Salvador Dalí expressed that the most profound visions can occur midway between waking and slumber, the "ten minutes before falling asleep," he stated. He called some such images *The Persistence of Memory*.

The painter Paul Cèzanne's art is described as "works that dance between reality and invention," invoking memory. Memory is the coming together of time, thought and emotion to present a viable image as a story. We acquire memories every moment, waking and asleep – the challenge is how we make use of them. Telling stories is one way of charting this unmapped territory, that place within memory, between fact and fantasy.

Where others might marshal the facts to tell the story, I make memories serve this purpose.

You will find here that memories and survival embrace. The stories that follow survive as memories. Others are last memorials.

Are these stories pure biography? No. Are they nonfiction? No. Though one or two are fantastic, they are all based on actual experiences and histories. It is for the reader to parse and filter them. The individual storytellers (there are twenty-four of them) don't censor themselves in their recitations and remembrances. Life's stories are not neat: they are complex, compelling, puzzling, and sometimes contradictory, as are our own lives. One of the characters in each story is time itself, acting as a mirror.

The Greeks believed "character is fate." A number of these stories say the reverse.

In daily use, the Italian word *verità* has two practical meanings – truth and also a version of the truth, as in "my *verità*, your *verità* and doubtless the various *verità* of others." Both meanings apply here. Italians often say that when two of them enter a room, they leave with four opinions. Readers may infer accordingly, and see that the unities of time and place may not align neatly.

Twenty-five hundred years ago, Aeschylus, the Greek poet and father of tragedy, taught that from despair comes "wisdom through the awful grace of god." This is the essence of the stories herein, colored by grace and filled with awe.

You will notice that several of the following stories are

about New Yorkers of Sicilian and Italian descent and African-Americans. That is because I am proudly descended from these people. I know them and I've been told their stories. But you will find others told here too. This is a mosaic of many colors, often intersecting. Survival comes in all shades, from all angles, all the time, and is worthy of reflection.

They have in common the universal truths, "love and honor and pity and pride and compassion and sacrifice." *

Anthony E. Shaw
Scarsdale, New York
December 31, 2020

*William Faulkner, Nobel Prize address, December 10, 1950

. . . no matter how long one peers in from the outside, it is never quite the view from within.

Peter Guralnick, *Careless Love* (1999)

CHAPTER ONE

Sunday Gravy with Uncle Del

Todt Hill, Staten Island, September 12, 1982

Two men sit facing each other and both of them are me.
Dr. R. D. Laing

"Uncle Del wants you to have Sunday Gravy with him. He's fixing it at his home on Todt Hill. You be there by noon. Okay?"

Uncle Del was a great man in my family. He loved his nieces and nephews and always made occasions to bring us together, like Sunday Gravy. He lived on Todt Hill, a four-hundred-foot elevation in the middle of Staten Island: the highest natural point in the five boroughs of New York City. Coincidentally, the highest unnatural point in the city was likewise on Staten Island, the Fresh Kills dump. The word in our family was Uncle Del may have contributed one or two bundles in the mountain of trash there. Person-sized bundles.

"Of course," I told my cousin, "my pleasure. I'm always happy to see my uncle." Whatever he may or may not have done, I loved my uncle. He didn't have to answer to me

3

about his life.

"Good. Good. We'll all be there."

Uncle Del was quite a cook. You ain't had Sunday Gravy until you had Uncle Del's. How could I say no?

If you are unfamiliar with Sunday Gravy, let me explain. *Sugo della domenica.* Where my people came from in Naples, Sunday was the day the whole family, great-grands to newborns, gathered in the home of the best cook to be together after Mass. The cook – it could be your mother or your aunt or an older cousin or your grandfather or uncle – would have started early in the morning or the night before. The six-day workweek meant Sunday was when families could relax, laugh, and enjoy a whole day together, sharing love. Love was expressed through the bounty of food and the caring hands of the cook. And the family's embrace. This tradition was brought to America.

First, the sauce. Skinned plum tomatoes crushed by hand, fruity Italian olive oil with a peppery kick, garlic, salt, basil, some chopped-up onions. Never olive oil from Greece or Spain or anywhere other than Italy. Some cooks left the onion whole and removed it after five or six hours simmering. No sugar – that was considered a sin. For sweetness, carrots or more onions were added. Maybe some red wine. Some cooks did, some cooks didn't.

Tomatoes and the garlic were the stars of the sauce that cooked for hours, the longer the better. The whole house was perfumed with a strong, deep acidic aroma. Bubbling gently, it became sweeter. It was both subtle and boldly flavored, a work of art.

What made it gravy were the meats that were fried and added in. Meatballs, but not giants; they were as big as a baby's fist, made with shredded dry bread soaked in milk and then squeezed, eggs, chopped beef and pork, more garlic, some parsley, and fresh grated cheese. Again, some cooks added chopped-up dried sausage like *soppressata* or ham. They made a hundred of these. Some were fried to be eaten by hand before the big meal; the rest were floated in the sauce. When it was time to be served, the fried meats, packages of beef or pork *braciole*, sweet sausage, pork ribs, sometimes meaty lamb bones or neck bones cooked in the sauce first, were served on a huge platter and covered in sauce.

Then there was the salad, extra large, with about everything green and ripe, olives too and peppers, onions, but no tomatoes. It was served in a huge, old, well-oiled wooden bowl, handed down and seasoned with garlic from generations of family cooks. This was dressed with homemade vinegar and some olive oil and salt. There were gorgeous tan loaves of bread, topped with sesame seeds and warm from the local bakery's oven. (No butter. We didn't use butter on bread. Butter was for baking.) We ate the salad and bread with the macaroni and gravy.

Enormous amounts of macaroni were cooked and lightly sauced. No Italian ever drowned the macaroni in sauce. On the side was cheese, Parmesan and Romano, grated at the table over your plate. Sometimes *ricotta salata*. The macaroni could be spaghetti or any pasta wide enough to hold the gravy, and it was served in very large bowls from which you helped yourself and added meats from the platter. One of the secrets to serving thick gravy over macaroni was to add a ladle of the pasta cooking water to the sauce before dishing it out; the starch from the pasta made the gravy stick better. You never rinsed the starch off the cooked macaroni for the same reason.

Red wine to drink, always red wine. We did not drink water with meals; in fact, we seldom drank plain water because the old folks didn't consider water very clean. "It rusts," grandma said. A prejudice they took with them from Naples to this country. Kids drank watered-down wine, with the water boiled first and then cooled to room temperature, or fruit juice or 7Up. A Sunday special that for a kid was worth waiting for.

After putting away the macaroni and gravy and the salad and bread, everybody relaxed, except the cook. He or she cleared the table for round two. We watched football on TV or swapped stories or looked at photo albums. In a couple of hours, we returned to the table to be greeted by more loaves of bread and the leftover meats, which we made into sandwiches. More wine, more laughing, and more eating.

The one outstanding part of all this was the nonstop talking and laughing. No meal was eaten in silence. Silence was not a virtue in my family. There were always six or seven conversations going on at once, loudly over one another. You would turn right and talk with your cousins' family, then turn left and talk with your brother, then look in front of you and gossip with your aunt and uncle. The talk never stopped.

About an hour or two later, out came the espresso and pastries, flaky shells called *sfogliatella*, biscotti, lemon cookies, on a big tray. And a big bowl of fresh fruit. I remember that to the old folks, the first ones to come over, the greatest delicacy was a banana. None of them had ever had a banana before coming to this country. You ate until your belly could hold no more. The remains were packed up and taken home by all. Two days' worth of meals in a few hours on Sunday. It was a blessing.

A tavola non s'invecchia: people did not get old at the table that was the center of the family's life!

This was family. This was love. This was Sunday Gravy. It lasted for hours, like lunch, snacks, dinner, and leftovers rolled into one meal. It was a tradition that held us together as Italians and Neapolitans.

That Sunday at Uncle Del's was no exception. *Cotto a puntino*: cooked to perfection. I was with my family. My uncle wore a white apron and a chef's hat. He was an older man, must have been seventy-five if he was a day, and he had a classy-looking toupee with black and gray streaks that were done naturally. He came out of the kitchen to say hello, carrying a big carving knife, for all the world looking like he was going to kill somebody, but his smile was so kind, you knew inside he was a sweetheart. He once was a bookie and shylock in the Bronx. Actually, the most active bookie on Arthur Avenue in the Bronx. Now he was mostly retired, collecting a pension from the New York City Parks Department, District Council 38. Not completely retired, though.

Decades ago, he was hired by Vic Silverbaum, the municipal union leader, to help organize the Parks Department employees, and in reward, he got a no-show job in Brooklyn's Prospect Park. His real job was taking betting action from the city workers and making payday loans. The feds came to the park, looking to find him committing the crime of bookmaking on government property. Unfortunately for them, Uncle Del was tipped off by a secretary in the local FBI office, a woman he was romancing after the death of his wife. When the agents found him, he was leaning on a rake like a dedicated gardener. That got them steamed, it was so obvious he was expecting them. They escorted him to their car and asked him what he was doing.

"Raking leaves," he answered.

"Really?" they responded "If you're a gardener, what do you call those little brown balls on the ground there?"

Uncle Del was ready. "Ginkgo nuts, but people call them 'stinko nuts' because when you step on them, they smell like crap."

The two feds looked at each other. He was right. They told him, "Get out of the car, wise guy," proving the FBI understood irony.

My uncle laughed all the way back to his rake. He told me that was the first and last time he picked up a gardening tool. Men like him weren't into manual labor, not like that.

I asked him about his early life. "Where I grew up in the Bronx," he said, "you had three career choices – laborer, priest, or gangster. I picked that last one."

Uncle Del said, "Everybody's got a scam. God gave the earth to the devil, so we can do what we want here." His view was apocalyptic: the devil ruled the world, it was evil, and living in it, Uncle Del would profit from it. I doubt he knew the meaning of "apocalyptic," but he lived it.

When I asked him why he was arrested by the feds for the first time, he said, "I loaned a guy some money. He couldn't pay me back, so I loaned him some more. That's why they pinched me." I consider these words of wisdom the official definition of criminality.

Uncle Del's second conviction was for making a threat using the telephone, violating the Hobbs Act. He told a guy he would "crack his head open" if he didn't pay the interest on a loan my uncle gave him. The truth was, Uncle Del knew it was a federal crime when he said it. "I knew my phone might be tapped, and I knew that telling him that was a crime. But I didn't control my temper. I gave the feds what they wanted. I pled no contest and took the time – eighteen months." Then he added, "Let that be a lesson. Hold your tongue and your temper. If you want to crack a guy's head, do it. Don't talk about it and you won't get caught."

He once told a story about a mob boss who found out his wife was having an affair with another gangster. The boss told my uncle to take care of it, meaning make him disappear. Uncle Del was fond of saying wistfully, "You know, people disappear every day. Nobody asks questions."

He began tailing this guy to learn his habits. People, even in the mob – perhaps especially in the mob – become so comfortable in their daily lives that they usually don't realize that consistency can be the difference between living and disappearing.

Uncle Del began following him around the clock. Unfortunately, Uncle Del's wife was used to him being home in the evenings. He was such a piece of bread (Italians say *buono come il pane,* as good as bread, because no one doesn't like bread) that my uncle didn't run around after work. When he became missing in action at home, his wife worried he was out cheating. She hired a private investigator, and the PI told her he would tail Uncle Del. The PI, however, knew my uncle and immediately told him about the wife's concerns. Uncle Del waited a week or two, getting the adulterer comfortable and complacent, before he disappeared. Good earner or not, made man or not, adultery with a mob boss's wife is a sure way to end up six feet under.

The third time Uncle Del was pinched, he was convicted on a federal rap and sent to prison in Marion, Ohio. What he was sentenced for was a pittance compared to what he was taking in with betting and loans. Before he went away, he settled his business at home – collecting outstanding debts, getting his customers paid up on time – before he turned the business over temporarily to one of his nephews. One debtor kept slipping away, ducking my uncle right up to prison time. If that wasn't bad enough, when Uncle Del was in prison the deadbeat started bragging about how he beat his loan. Dumb. I don't know what you know about federal prisons, but for the most part, they're a stopping point. You go in, do your time, and come out, same as when you left. The last thing a civilian should do is mock someone in prison. He will be back on the street.

When Uncle Del got out he already heard about the deadbeat's boasts. Now, a made man can't have a civilian damage his reputation. It is bad for business and a major disgrace. Uncle Del decided right away that the money was less important than his reputation. The loudmouth's body was found behind a dumpster, with his tongue cut out, a clear message. My uncle was no more than a month back from what men like him called "school," and he was once again in the life.

Uncle Del's sustenance, his bread and salt, was sports gambling: from college basketball to pro football. This was the exquisite high he provided to his most dedicated customers: the degenerate gamblers.

A degenerate gambler is the lifeblood of a bookie and a shylock: a willing victim. Degenerates, you can always tell who they are. They hustle for a living even if they are well paid because every dime goes to the bookie. Football, basketball, cards, lottery, Joker Poker, numbers, the works. When a degenerate starts to bet, he never stops. He can't stop. It's in his genes. His future is more betting action, getting that high. The kids are lost to him, his wife is meaningless, he can't hold a job though he might be super talented, the house falls apart, and the mortgage is foreclosed. The kids' college fund is exhausted. Still he bets. He can't afford to eat or wash his clothes, and still he bets. The degenerate is hooked on a powerful drug. That high becomes more elusive and diminished over time.

He bets money he doesn't have, then the shylock takes over. He sticks a needle in the degenerate's vein and pumps out all the blood. That is their relationship. When there is no more blood, the shylock sells the skin. Finally, he collects the soul. Once the degenerate can't bet anymore because he's out of credit, in over his head with the bookie and the shylock, banned from anyone taking his bets, he dies. Many a family has been utterly destroyed by such a loser. Once he positively can't make good on his debts, he is often gone, useless to himself and everybody else. Degenerate gamblers paid my uncle's mortgage and financed his new cars. They put food on his table, the clothes on his back, and the gifts in my pocket.

He gave the degenerates what they hungered and lusted for: action. He turned desire into desperate need.

A few times, I visited my uncle when he was paying his bills. Like everything else about him, paying bills was unique. See, he didn't believe in putting his serious money in a bank, where the government and the FBI and the IRS could find out what he had. Now, his pension checks went into a bank account, but his real money was kept in cash in his house. On bill-paying day, I would find my uncle seated at the dining room table with separate stacks of cash in front of him, allocating for each bill: the gas, the power company, the telephone, and so on. He paid in cash and in person. Years after my uncle passed, I discovered that one of my friends had been his paperboy. "Your uncle would tip me ten bucks for a dollar fifty delivery charge." Uncle Del was generous in many ways. He always had time for me to tell him my problems. He listened, with love.

He had a gravelly voice that he kept low, like a half-whisper, so taping what he said wasn't easy or clear to understand. For example, the feds said in court papers that he became a made man in 1947. Wrong. What he told me in private was that he was formally inducted when he was forty-seven years old, in 1976. The feds never corrected themselves on that, but I knew the truth. I learned that a whole lot of what the feds said and swore to under oath was false.

What I appreciated about my uncle was that most of the time, he didn't have to do anything to get what he wanted. His look, the way he looked, what people knew about him, the way he spoke were usually intimidating enough.

He was once having lunch with the deputy mayor of Yonkers. The deputy mayor and Uncle Del were friends. Nothing crooked, they liked each other. They're having lunch, talking, and in comes one of the young men who worked for the city, a union member. He sees the two of them leave their table to walk out and Uncle Del and the deputy mayor hug and kiss on the cheek, like two old Italian friends. This bigmouth goes back to work and tells everyone the deputy mayor kissed a mobster in public! Word gets back to my uncle. He finds out when the smartass is at that restaurant next. Uncle Del walks up to the table, stands over him, and says, "You know who I am?" The guy is petrified with fear, frozen. Uncle Del repeats, "You know who I am? You got something to say to me?" He doesn't have to raise his voice. His look is more than enough. "You want to talk about me, you do it to my face." Then my uncle leaves. The city worker is so frightened, he can't finish his lunch. He goes to the toilet and throws up. All Uncle Del did was look and talk.

Another time, my uncle and the deputy mayor were lunching with a famous local politician, a man who had been a mayor, county executive, and lieutenant governor. He became a local TV commentator and was a harsh critic of the mayor's administration. The purpose of the lunch was to try to convince this man to cool it with the criticisms. He was adamant – "I tell it like I see it," he says. He left the table for the restroom. Uncle Del followed. Five minutes later, the man returned to the table and announced, "I need to be fairer to you folks." When lunch ended, the deputy mayor drew Uncle Del aside and asked, "What did you do to him?" My uncle replied, "He knows who I am."

I realize my portrait of him is a paradox. During one of his last appearances in federal court, the judge sternly admonished the US attorney, "No person on trial in my court, who fought on D-Day, will be denied bail." With that, she ordered my uncle to wear an ankle bracelet to track his whereabouts before sentencing. He had volunteered to fight in World War II and piloted a landing craft onto Omaha Beach. "The water was red all around me," he remembered. Why did he lie about his age and volunteer at sixteen? "Because of what the Germans were doing to the Jews." He hung his D-Day participation certificate on his living room wall proudly. I contrast this with the fact that a week after he started wearing the court ordered ankle bracelet, he complained to the US marshals that it was cutting off the circulation to his foot. "I'm an old man with high blood pressure," he told them. The bracelet was removed and he went back to doing his business – while awaiting sentencing for a conviction! That was Uncle Del.

He was an understated man of few words. What words he used were choice. He had the enviable ability, though it was more an extraordinary gift than a skill, to listen quietly to any number of people speak and afterward describe each one's core personality: who was a liar, who could be trusted, which one was reliable, and which was full of bull. It was his impressive gift, and he would regale me with his insights. They always proved accurate and priceless.

He appreciated wisdom, in all its forms. He instructed me, "Never forget, women are sharper than men, mentally. They see things that we don't see. And they don't brag. I knew a guy who came home one night, went to the bedroom, and sat on the bed to take off his shoes. His wife was watching him. When he took off his pants and socks, she called him a cheating bastard! He was dumbstruck because he had been out with his girlfriend, but how could his wife have known? She eyed him up and down and said, 'You're not smart. There are no rings around your ankles where your socks were pinching your legs! That means, you tomcat, you didn't have your socks on all night!'"

What a man he was. My memories of him are not

exaggerated. They're dear and true. I miss him and think about him nearly every day. I still hear his voice.

Uncle Del was a bookmaker, shylock, union corrupter, debt collector, and a stone-cold gangster. He lived his life. Old age and dementia took him before he was convicted for a fourth time. He died in a lonely hospital bed with the FBI at his side: a tragedy. That was my uncle. What sins he had were not mine to judge. He loved me and his whole family. I miss his Sunday Gravy and the warmth that came with it. He was my uncle and a wonderful one at that. I cherish my memories of him. May he rest in peace. I hope to see him again, both of us free of our pasts.

CHAPTER TWO

Out of the Sky

Park Slope, Brooklyn, December 16, 1960

Luck is a very thin wire between survival and disaster.
Hunter S. Thompson

December 16, 1960 was almost two months after my thirteenth birthday and nine days before Christmas. It was a Friday, with wet snow falling in the morning. The heat in our home wasn't working and my father went to work late, staying home until the furnace was back on. The snow turned into light freezing rain and fog around ten o'clock. My mother didn't begin thinking about taking me to school until after then. She was worried about the cold outside and the possibility that our water pipes might freeze without heat in the apartment.

A bit after 10:30, maybe closer to 10:36 that morning, she and I were about to step off our apartment building's stoop when we heard an explosion. It shook the ground, louder than any noise I'd ever heard. It was frightening not solely because it was so loud but because it felt like a bomb hit nearby, with the startling shaking. She and I stopped and looked around to try and figure it.

Right after the explosion, there was silence. People from our building and the others on our block were rushing out onto the street. No one knew what happened, and everyone was scared.

It took less than five minutes for us to find out.

A woman stuck her head out of a ground-floor window of the apartment building directly across the street from us and shouted, "Plane crash! There's a plane crash on Seventh Avenue!"

All of us on the street started running to Seventh Avenue, and people in their homes began yelling the latest news from their radios out to us in the street.

"Seventh and Sterling!"

"It's a big plane full of people!"

"The Pillar of Fire was hit!"

The Pillar of Fire was a church at Seventh Avenue and Sterling Place. There was no love lost for it in this neighborhood. The church used to host the Ku Klux Klan and preach against Jews, blacks, and, especially stupidly in this neighborhood, Catholics. Frankly, all the Italians, Irish, and Puerto Ricans despised the Pillar.

The streets were cold and wet, with gray piles of dirty snow. Snow from early that morning put a coating on the sidewalk trash. Mist hung in the air. The closer we got to the scene, the heavier the smell of burnt fuel and the increasing panic of the neighborhood.

A disaster this big now would be cordoned off by the cops and firefighters; back then, we got close enough to the wreck to touch the pieces of the plane strewn on the street and sidewalk.

Two large airplanes had clipped each other's wings in

the sky, knocking off engines and sending both into death spirals. One, a TWA propellor plane, crashed in Staten Island, in a nonresidential area called Miller's Field. That plane's nickname was *Star of Sicily*. The other, a United DC-8, plowed into Seventh and Sterling, which was heavily residential with many brick apartment buildings like ours. Ten buildings were destroyed.

The pilots steered the falling plane away, by a few feet, from a Catholic high school, St. Augustine's. A teacher there said he saw the doomed pilots' eyes as they tilted the wing, trying not to hit the school. That sounded dubious. A student learned that the rest of his family had been in one room in their apartment, the one room that wasn't destroyed in their home. A family saved twice was a double miracle. One guy I know claims he was there at St. Augustine's, in the classroom that day. He boasts that he looked out the window, despite his teacher's warning, to stare at the approaching plane. "I got glass in my eye," according to him. There is neither a record of him being in school then nor any of his being treated for a resulting injury. BS. He is, in fact, Baron Münchhausen. The memories of a tragedy attract liars and bullthrowers, seeking notoriety.

Everyone on both planes was killed; some in the plane that crashed in Brooklyn were killed along the way when the two planes met and touched structures on the way down. Except for an eleven-year-old boy who landed in a snow bank. He was alive enough to make it to Methodist Hospital before he died the next day. His lungs were burned by the flaming jet fuel. In his pocket were four dimes and five nickels. He died with sixty-five cents. His father was a successful businessman back in Ohio, who took his son to the airport that morning.

With my mother, I saw the wreckage all over the place; giant pieces of the wings and fuselage with the name United printed on them in blue, the engines, luggage, kids' toys, and wrapped Christmas packages. Bodies strapped in seats. Hands, feet, and heads in the gutter like discarded basketballs and trash bags. The pilot, his mouth and eyes wide open, trapped in the cockpit. He was dead, though a cop tried to get his body out with an ax.

The mayor, Wagner, was on the scene with the fire commissioner. I had never seen them in person before. My mom and I were too spellbound by the enormous tragedy to pay much attention to anything other than the gruesome spectacle before us. Our neighborhood was changed forever by the shock of this larger than life tragedy. The memories of Park Slope would never be the same.

The Pillar of Fire was on fire, completely. One old man, the caretaker, was asleep in the church at the time. He died instantly. Apart from him, nobody mourned that church. We thought, *Good riddance and rot in hell.*

Five others on the ground were killed instantly: a garbage man who was clearing away the snow, a local butcher, a doctor out walking his dog, and two men who were selling Christmas trees on the corner. Dead in a fiery instant. Alive one moment, burnt to a crisp the next. There were dozens of stretchers holding bodies with blankets over them. The street was clogged with firehoses, snaking around the asphalt like giant pythons congregating.

I read much later that one of the passengers predicted her own death. A college girl dreamed she would die in that plane. She even told her boyfriend he wouldn't see her again.

I wondered then, how does something this terrible happen? Over one hundred and thirty lives gone in seconds. *Why some people and not others?* A famous climber who was the first European to reach the summit of Mount Everest arrived at the airport too late to catch the flight. He lived to the age of eighty-eight. *How was it decided*, I asked myself, *that some would die and the rest would live?* Was there a plan, a book maybe that said who would go when and somehow those doomed would all be in the same place, while others would avoid that place or be stopped from going before their time? St. Augustine's was spared and the Pillar of Fire burned to the ground.

You have to understand, for a thirteen-year-old about to celebrate Christmas, these were important questions. I needed to know, *What do you call this plan? Who decided it?* It couldn't be the God we were taught about in church. He wouldn't do something like this. To an eleven-year-old boy who never hurt anyone? No, something else caused this. Maybe the devil? Was the devil in charge sometimes?

All through that Christmas, I carried those images from Seventh Avenue and Sterling Place with me. A huge burned engine. Undelivered Christmas packages with wrapping that was now covered in the soot of jet fuel. A boy in the snow. How does this happen? Why?

CHAPTER THREE

We're Done

Midtown East, Manhattan, June 13, 1969

*All concerns of men go wrong when they wish
to cure evil with evil.*
Sophocles

The Lounge was where they all hung out. The stars, the wannabes, the soon to be once-weres, drunks, gamblers, hoods, hangers-on, dames, pretty young women and their dates, made men, shady characters, flirts, come-on artists, Yankee sluggers, college kids, Super Bowl quarterbacks, the lucky few.

It had music and dancers and famous spareribs.

Every evening was a rock and roll party. The host was Izzie Silver. Izzie was partners with two other men, Silent Eddie and Rocco Scali. Rocco was known as "Mr. Green" because he made a lot of it. The joint was protected by someone else, Tommy Tombstone (he once hid some stolen swag under a tombstone). Mr. Green was the boss. Silent Eddie was from Philly. He was the quiet type.

They were four moral misfits. Izzie was calm and unemotional. When he met a person, he calculated what he could gain by killing or not killing him. It was a matter of pure dollars and cents on Izzie's ledger, and he planned accordingly. Silent Eddie disliked arguments. For his own peace of mind, conflicts were resolved in short order, up or down, dead or alive. He had to have life set right quickly. Mr. Green's life was one generally removed from firsthand violence because violence could potentially interfere with his ability to earn. He favored delegating unpleasantries to men like Tommy, though Mr. Green would take part when he felt strongly about the outcome. Tommy was as base a human being as one could ever imagine. Killing was a thrill for him, but he wasn't sloppy or impetuous. He enjoyed taking orders and doing his duty. Together, they made a productive, successful team running a lucrative business, among other things. They were the leftovers of humanity; the garbage floating in the river, in the wake of the tugboat of human life.

The Lounge was a go-go bar in the front and it served tasty spareribs in the back room. Men played liar's poker at the bar. The back part was for gangsters and their close friends. For a time, it was the place to be in the city. Izzie was the one everybody trusted. Tommy sat at the bar and made sure no one and nothing got out of hand.

Nowadays, maybe three or four people, at most, know these stories. They're told by a certain man, who heard it from another man who was many years ago in deep with Mr. Green, and they're true.

Mr. Green was as tough as they come but no nonsense. He said that once a skinny black kid came into one of his nightclubs, asking for a job. The kid was thin as a rail and wore high-water pants, must have been four inches above his shoes. Mr. Green took one look and told him to get out.

The kid came back several times, asking for work singing, but he was told to get out every time. The kid was Johnny Mathis.

Mr. Green did business with Gigi the Jet. The Jet had an apartment in the Hassler Hotel in Rome. He would jet into Rome, buy a few suits and shoes, have dinner, and jet back home to New York. The Jet. Mr. Green disliked Gigi. He really hated him, but they did business. Money is money, and the Jet made a ton of money.

Away from the Lounge, Mr. Green had a little social club, a place where he could play cards, cook some lunch, relax, and be with his friends out of the spotlight and away from the prying eyes of the FBI. His social club was the Veterans Army Navy Store, a few side blocks east from the Lounge. This was a store with no merchandise. The windows were soaped up so no one could see inside. An old man, Mr. Russo, who was eighty, sat in a chair behind the window, peering out through a small part of the glass that wasn't soaped up, looking to see if anybody was casing the place. Inside were some old chairs and tables, a bar, a jukebox, and hooks on the walls to hang coats and hats. Everybody at the club wore a hat. There was a small kitchen where Mr. Green cooked. He was a very good cook.

Mr. Green stopped by the kitchen of the best steakhouse in New York, a place with sawdust on the floor and cartoons on the walls. He got five big lobsters and took them back to the Veterans to make *zuppa di pesce*, seafood soup. He would cook the lobster and use the tail meat in the soup with mussels, clams, and shrimp. The shrimp and lobster shells and the shrimp heads made the broth. Chop up some onions, green peppers, celery, carrots, and tomatoes, add some white wine, a lot of garlic and basil, and some parsley and red pepper flakes. Simmer. Seafood goes in last. Toast some bread with olive oil and garlic to go with it. A lot of work over the stove, but it tasted out of this world.

The soup was ready and in walked the Jet. "Smells good. I'm hungry," the Jet announced. Mr. Green picked up the pot of soup, poured it in the garbage, and replied "It's no good. Sorry."

For laughs, the men at the Veterans stole Mr. Russo's cane, removed the rubber tip, and whittled a half-inch off the bottom, then replaced the tip and put it back on the chair. A couple of weeks later they asked Mr. Russo why he was so bent over. He said, "I don't know. I guess I'm shrinking." To them, this was big humor.

One day at the Lounge, Izzie was holding down the door when two nobodies walked in, guys Izzie never saw before. They were young, maybe in their early thirties, trying to be gangsters. They told Izzie, "You need new management in this joint. We're the new managers." Izzie told them, "I'm an employee here. You're going to have to talk to the owners. They'll be back tonight, around seven." They left and returned at seven, like the idiots they were.

Sure enough, Silent Eddie and Mr. Green were there and told them they would all talk downstairs. The two mopes followed Mr. Green to the basement, where the kitchen prep work was done. Silent Eddie followed behind the mopes. When he passed the meat prep room, Silent Eddie grabbed a meat cleaver. He brought it down on the second mope's head, chopping it neatly in two. The other mope turned around to see his partner's brains on the basement floor. Mr. Green turned to him and said with a smile, "We're done. You can go now."

The surviving mope ran like hell out of the place. Mr. Split Brains was stripped and dumped in the used grease barrel and probably wound up in a bar of Ivory soap, washing someone's balls. Mr. Green, who had lived through the Great Depression, gave the dead mope's wristwatch to his grandson for Christmas, on the principle of waste not, want not.

CHAPTER FOUR

A Lesson Learned

Belmont, The Bronx, November 22, 1963

The sum of a million facts is not the truth.
William Manchester

When I was fourteen years old, my family moved to Arthur Avenue in the Bronx. My new neighborhood was a lot like my old one. Italian families, meaning mother and father together in one house with their kids; grandma and grandpa on the same block, if not in the same house.

Every family knew every other family. We all attended the same church, Our Lady of Mount Carmel, and confessed to the same priest, Father Loretti. We bought our groceries from the same neighborhood stores – Biancardi for meat; Teitel Brothers for cheese and spices (everyone called them "the Jews"); Madonia Brothers for bread and sweets. We probably all ate the same meals on the same days of the week. Chicken on Monday, raviolis on Tuesday, spaghetti on Wednesday, soup on Thursday, fish on Friday, *trippa con patate* on Saturday, macaroni and gravy on Sunday.

My parents spoke a lot of Italian at home and to me. Every other kid's parents did the same, but they wanted us to be Americans. American we learned in school and on the street. My grandmother, who lived with us, never learned a great deal of English: she would sit in a chair in the neighborhood vegetable market and listen to the American names of produce, and then copy the sounds to order in English. At home, she spoke Italian.

The kids I hung out with were almost all Italians. That was my block, all Italian families. Two streets away was an apartment building that was all Irish. Go figure. I guess one Irisher moved in and brought the rest of them. You'd think the Italians would clash with the Irish. Sometimes, but not really. We kids were rivals, especially in sports, but we stood on our block and they stood on theirs. Each of us proud of who we were and determined to keep it that way.

Except in the Irish building, they had a super who lived with his family in the basement apartment. He was a Puerto Rican, Mr. Dominquez. We always called him "Mr. D." He was a wonderful adult, loved kids, didn't care what nationality you were. In the summers, he would bring out the hose and spray us kids in the heat. He had a son, Robby, and Robby was an ace baseball player, miles ahead of the rest of us neighborhood boys. He could pitch, he could throw, he was fast, he could catch, and he could hit a ball, a regulation baseball, a mile. He told us his nickname was "Roberto," after Roberto Clemente.

The problem was, both us Italians and the Irishers wanted him on our pickup baseball teams. We said he was an Italian because he was tan-skinned like us. They said he lived in their building so he was honorary Irish. He said the Puerto Ricans in New York were like the Irish in

Britain. That I didn't understand, but I expect his father had said it to him. This was a problem. I finally solved it by having him traded back and forth between our two teams. One week he was Italian, the next, Irish. The team he was on that week won. He didn't care, just so he got to play.

When I returned years later to look at the building where I lived from grammar through high school, I realized how cramped and beat-up it was. The hallways smelled of cooking, like years of fried garlic and onions in olive oil. The accents were Spanish and the staple was rice now, not pasta. The windows were crooked and the stoop was falling apart. It looked like it did fifty years ago. It hadn't changed. I had. Now it was filled with other families and they attended Mount Carmel, like I had. When I was a little kid, my home was the best place I knew. It is a pleasant memory.

I went to Mount St. Michael Academy for middle school. The school's dean was Mr. D'Onofrio, the principal Father Lynch, and the parish priest Father Santonocito.

In school one of my friends was Mikey. We weren't in the same homeroom so I didn't know his last name. He was Mikey from the next block. Mikey liked the same things in life I did, like flipping cards. He and I were flipping them one day and having a good time too. Jack on the deuce. King on the jack. Aces over everything. Apparently so good that a neighbor heard us hollering and called Mikey's mother. She caught us. To my surprise, she was Mrs. Dolan, my friendly homeroom teacher. She was particularly angry because I was leading her little boy down the road to hell with the devil's pasteboards. She let me know it, and I'm sure Mikey caught a whipping. Good thing she didn't know about the bottles of beer Mikey stole from his fridge and he and I drank in the playground on the sly.

My father found out soon enough about the game but when I got home, he took me aside. Instead of being angry at me, he told me, "You was playing cards with Mrs. Dolan's son? I really don't care. Cards is a game. You didn't cheat him, did you?" I answered no, we weren't betting, just flipping cards for fun. He put his hand on my shoulder and said, "Cards never killed anybody. Don't play cards with Mikey, okay?" I answered yes dutifully and noticed my father didn't tell my mom. I guessed cards were for men like my father who didn't mind a little fun. Mrs. Dolan, however, never gave me a smile in school again.

A little over a month after my fifteenth birthday, November 22, 1963, I was in homeroom class at the end of the school day. Ask anyone of my generation and that person can tell you where he or she was and what was happening when the news came. That date is burned into our memory. It remains a black hole in my otherwise mostly regular childhood.

The principal called everyone, teachers too, into the auditorium to tell us and lead us in prayer.

Catholics took it particularly hard. In his way, he was one of all of us, Italian, Irish, Spanish, bonded by our shared memories of the Church. He attended Mass five days before.

My mother and father adored him. My father never voted because he thought that would bring him to the government's attention, but if he had, he would have voted twice for the first Catholic president. What they didn't know about him is what is known now. The adultery. The sex games in the White House with young women staffers. The day after his assassination, my parents hung his photo from the front page of the *Daily News* in our home. Every family on our block did the same.

He had a pretty, faithful wife and two beautiful children. He ran around with any skirt he fancied. This now seems so dirty, such a betrayal of ordinary peoples' love for him. All right, a powerful man in a position like his might have a mistress. Even the Church wouldn't begrudge him a mistress. But he was reckless. I've looked at him sideways since time has revealed his true nature.

But back then, on that day I was shocked and saddened and confused. How could this happen in America? My parents thought the same thoughts. This was our country, our stable, shining country. Better than all the other countries in the world. We don't kill our leaders. Something inside of me, in my heart, broke that day and never healed. I now knew anything could happen, people get killed all the time; people, well-known people, people a kid depended on to be safe and strong, could die in an instant. The world was from then on a different place. If someone wanted you dead badly enough, you died. You had to be on your guard to stop them before they stopped you. If a president could be shot dead, anyone could.

That day was filled with lessons learned for me, ones I carry with me to this day. Don't take life for granted. Be prepared to fight for your life all the time. Beware of people's adoration of you. You always have enemies. Always be suspicious.

One other thing that happened about the time I was in high school, maybe I was fifteen or sixteen, that still stands out in my memory. It was a holiday, Columbus Day or something like that. School was closed. I went with my mother to Mass, then to the market. There she met Mrs. Zingalli, one of the neighborhood ladies. I wandered off. Mr. and Mrs. Zingalli lived around the corner from us. Decent people, soft-spoken, kept to themselves. They didn't have children. Their last name, Zingalli, was Romani, meaning their family were or once were gypsies.

By the time I found my way back to my mother, she finished her conversation with Mrs. Zingalli. We went home and the *pasta fagioli* was prepared. Father came home from the fish market and we sat down to dinner. Mother started telling us about what she and our neighbor talked about.

"Mrs. Zingalli told me a story today. Back in Taormina, she and her younger sister lived alone on a tiny farm. Their parents died in the war. All they had was each other. Her younger sister had a man, a fiancé. They were to be married and Mrs. Zingalli, well she wasn't Mrs. Zingalli then, would live with them, her sister and brother-in-law. One day an old woman stopped at the farm and asked for some bread. Mrs. Zingalli told her they had no bread, but she could give her some fried zucchini and olive oil. The old lady took the food and said she would tell her fortune. Mrs. Zingalli asked if she would ever be married, after all here was her younger sister with a fiancé and Mrs. Zingalli already twenty-eight and never married. The old lady told her, 'The cat hasn't walked on the roof. The tile hasn't fallen. Your luck hasn't arrived yet. It will.'

"The old lady left and Mrs. Zingalli didn't understand anything, except she was lonely. The next day, she and her sister were sitting outside their house, peeling potatoes. A cat ran up one of their olive trees, chasing a bird. The bird flew away and the cat jumped on the roof following it. He knocked a roof tile that came loose and the cat and the tile fell. They both hit the sister in the head, killing her right there. Mrs. Zingalli was overcome with grief. The sister's fiancé consoled her. Then he married her, made her Mrs. Zingalli, and brought her here to America."

Father was eating his soup and listening. He stopped and looked at my mother and me.

"Gypsies" he said. "They see the future. The old lady was a gypsy. Mr. Zingalli is a gypsy. They can see their fate. But look, no children. Fate cuts both ways."

I didn't say another word all evening before I went to bed. I kept hearing my father's words about fate. I was shaken. This explained things. So, I thought, that's it. Fate, there was no way to stop it. The president. The cat, the bird, the sister, Mrs. Zingalli, they shared a fate. They had to do what they did. Fate was kind and cruel at the same time. It opened the way for some, closed it for others. After that story, I knew my future was a question mark, be what it may. It wasn't what my parents thought it should be. I had a different dream. Another place in life. My own place. My own future and nobody else's. Fate was an individual acquaintance you never really knew.

The lesson was magnified when my class studied the Gospels, guided by Father Santonocito. In Matthew, Luke, and John, Judas is described as being foreordained to betray Christ. There is a description of him possessed by Satan. The more we studied Judas, the more I sympathized with the poor bastard. He had no choice. He was going to hell the day he was born. If he hadn't betrayed Jesus, someone else would have had to. Judas got a raw deal. His fate was to be the worst of the worst, the lowest of the low.

But wait – I reasoned what Judas did, fulfilling his fate, caused the Lord to come into His time and be glorified. Wasn't that a good thing? Without Judas's rotten fate, we would not be saved. I wondered, was Judas forgiven? He should have been. I was positive he was. Mrs. Zingalli didn't kill her sister. Fate did. Judas was on the same lousy boat. Such was his fate.

This was one of those basic turning points. I faced the ultimate unknown – the rest of my life. Should I be scared? Should I worry about things I couldn't see or feel until they were in front of me? Every minute ahead was a surprise. What I would do or was done to me was a mystery, the biggest mystery of all: the future that was always one second next. I liked puzzles, and this one was unsolvable for the moment because I had no idea what it was. Except for gypsies, I guess, no one could solve them in the here and now. Many, many years later, I read the story of the greatest Greek dramatist, who wrote tragedies. Walking along a beach, he was hit on the head and killed by a turtle, dropped by a vulture. What a twist of fate!

I pondered this mass of unanswered questions at the ripe old age of fifteen or sixteen. What was I to do with this knowledge?

I decided I was going to live to the fullest. There didn't appear to be any other way; for damn sure I wasn't going to roll up in a ball to wait for what I couldn't see! In fact, I was liberated by it all. I had choices! My door was unlocked. I wasn't held back by what might happen next. I was opened to live! Live and take my best shot. The future, and who could say what that would be, wasn't chained to me or me to it, as far as I could tell. The future wasn't a memory to taunt me: it was always an empty page. How could I be held by a thing I didn't know and couldn't see? I would meet it later. I was now. Fate would have to kiss my ass because I was going to be in front of it.

If it was a race, I would do what it took to finish first every day, because I was headed in some direction or another, no matter what. Consequences? Could it be true that whatever I did in life, if it was going to happen anyway, I could be forgiven? I bet poor Judas got a pass upstairs; it would certainly be fair, and I was certain the Big Guy was fair. I wasn't going to kill anyone or like that. Short of that extreme, I figured I was home free. Live!

Thus, I began to know how to play the game of life, and all hesitation and regret became unimportant. I trusted my judgment and let the rest unfold. If I couldn't tell where it would lead, nobody else could either. It's worked for me, so far.

CHAPTER FIVE

Under the Arch

Prospect Park, Brooklyn, June 28, 1971

Those to whom evil is done, do evil in return.
W. H. Auden

"All right, Danny, I'll tell him. A - I - D stands for American Italian Defense. I got this idea from a Jew rabbi, who made a lot of sense about defending his people. Here, read this."

Joey Alessandra was listening to the Boss of his Family explain their latest business venture.

Mr. John Carfano took a folded sheet of paper from his pocket and handed it to Joey unfolded. At the top in big black capitals was "**AMERICAN ITALIAN DEFENSE**." Underneath were five lines in bold black type:

Love of your people and heritage
Dignity and pride
Iron
Discipline and Unity
Indestructibility

Joey read it and asked, "What does all this mean?"

"You see! No Italian in America thinks like this. This Jew, Kahane, is standing up for his people and making them stand up for themselves. We Italians in this country have to do the same. We let people look down on us, make fun of us, call us 'guinea,' 'wop,' 'dago.' We're a joke with our funny accents and garlic and meatballs. We have to practice being proud of being Italian. Love our heritage. Carry ourselves with dignity. Fight for Italians to be respected. Why is every crime blamed on Italians? You risked your life for your country in Vietnam. Should anyone be allowed to call you a dago?"

"Hell no," Joey answered.

"Hell no. But you see this disrespect everywhere. On TV, in the movies. In the damn movies!"

Joey read about a protest the Boss started about movies that showed Italians as criminals and lowlifes. Not that he and Joey weren't gangsters, but the ones on the movie screen were cheap hoods. They couldn't speak English. They beat up their women. They killed innocent bystanders. Those things the two of them and their associates were not.

"I started AID to fight back for all Italian-Americans. Enough already. I've got respectable businessmen on our side. Jew politicians. Newspaper editors. Sports stars. This is becoming a nationwide movement."

Out of the corner of his eye, Joey saw his Cousin Danny wincing ever so slightly. This didn't sound like a gangster's business, civil rights. That was for Martin Luther King, and he got clipped because of it. Joey didn't know who this Jew Kahane was, but he was sure the Jew would get clipped too if he stood out too much. Gangsters stayed under the radar. They didn't call attention to themselves. Though Joey loved Mr. Carfano, this did not sound promising. Who would pay them to march around with a sign saying "Italian Civil Rights"?

Mr. Carfano was revved up about this. "See, Joe, we have to get people behind us for support. When they do, especially businesses, they'll pay us to defend their rights. We don't need to demand money when our supporters will give it because they agree with what we're doing. Other people will pay to get on the right side."

This seemed like a good point but glancing at his cousin's face, Joey could see he didn't agree, but he had to go along with the Boss.

"I've got businesses signed up as dues-paying sponsors of AID. The other Families are behind me. We've got our organizers on the streets. Already we have one hundred thousand members."

Joey dared to ask, "What if this thing gets too big? Will we have the time to take care of our regular business? What if another Family decides we're too loud or they want a piece of it?" Having killed Vietcong regularly for the last eighteen months, Joey wasn't afraid to speak up. He hoped Mr. Carfano would see this wasn't him being insubordinate. Joey had genuine questions.

"Joey, I like the way you think. We have to look out for all those things. But all the businesses we're in, we have the same concerns. This is a new territory for us, and we're the first. I need you to be a part of this. It's growing. I know you're not happy at your club. For the time being, while I look for the right man to take it over, I'll need you there, but I also need you to represent AID in that neighborhood. Your neighbors there love you; they've been asking about you for a year and a half. Can I count on you to go back and hold that down for the Family while we grow this thing?"

What doubts Joey might have, when the Boss asks, you do.

"Yes, Mr. Carfano, you can count on me. I'm with you."

"You're a good kid, Joey. You and Danny can look at the other things you want to pursue." He looked at Danny. "You talk to Joey about those bingo parlors in Florida?"

"Not yet. I wanted him to talk to you first and get your blessing."

Mr. Carfano replied, "My blessing? Come here, Joey. You always have my blessing!"

They all stood and the Boss hugged Joey.

Joseph John Alessandra was a South Brooklyn boy. South Brooklyn really wasn't the southern part of Brooklyn. On the map, it was the western part. Back when Brooklyn was a city, western Brooklyn was south of the city hall (now Borough Hall) of the City of Brooklyn. Thus, it became South Brooklyn. Joey's heritage was Sicilian on his father's side and Naples from his mother's family. Joey's Cousin Danny, on his father's side, was an established earner in the Carfano Family. Danny was next to Mr. Carfano everywhere.

Joey's father was a World War II veteran and a dockworker, a totally legitimate man. He was like most Italians in America, then and now, clean as a whistle. He knew what was going on in his neighborhood, even among his own relatives and nearest family. He didn't judge, but he chose to be legit. He was a wonderful man, a loving husband, and a good father. His whole family was Sicilian, from a mountain town near the Salso River, for as long as anyone knew. He was the fourth generation in America. In their home, what Joey's father said was gospel. You better not question it. He didn't have to speak. A look from him was enough to tell you what you could and could not do. An absolute dictator, but with love.

His mother was a saint. Every Italian little boy of Joey's generation called his mother that. That was what Italian mothers were, saints. Her people were from the *quartieri* of Barra in Naples. She was third generation. She attended Mass every day. She said novenas. She was faithful to the Church and her family. She was a loving parent and a supportive, loving wife. In her whole life, she did no wrong. She never put the *malocchio,* the evil eye, on anyone, though there were times she wanted to. She wasn't into *pettegolare*, gossiping like many of the older neighborhood women were. Her constant refrain was "pray the rosary, ask God, and be patient," from Padre Pio. She was gentle but strong.

When Joey was twelve, in the fall of 1964, his father came home from work on the docks earlier than usual. His father's life was centered on three things: his family, his Church, and his job. Each one of these things supported the other two. This was stability and security. You could call it the greatness of America. He had no real property – these three things were his solitary property in life. He felt blessed.

He came home early and on his face was a thing Joey had never seen before. He was frightened. At such an early age, Joey knew his father was suddenly frightened of something, for the first time that Joey could tell. His father made no attempt to hold back from his family what was going on.

"I'm losing my job." He looked at them both directly and said it. He might have said, "I'm losing my life."

Joey's mother asked, "What do you mean? How can you lose your job? The docks aren't closing, are they?" She held Joey's hand, listening. The father's fear had spread to her. To see this giant of a man, her husband, in this state, almost broken by fear, was more than she could comprehend by herself. She held her son's hand so that she didn't collapse on the spot.

"The dock boss, he tells me I'm being replaced. Replaced by a young man. I think his nephew. I think just here from Palermo. His nephew to replace me. I'm not needed anymore."

"Frank, you have a union. Talk to the union. They can't do this."

"The boss, he's in with the union. The union is no help. I'm done."

Joey forever gave his mother all the credit for what she did next. She didn't crumble. A power, a force shot through her. Physically shot through her body. Joey felt it in her hand. Not letting go, she walked over to the phone calmly. She picked up the receiver and, balancing it on her shoulder and cheek, dialed. Somehow, maybe part of the force in her told Joey, through their hands held together, who she was calling.

"Danny, we need you." That was all she said. No hello. No goodbye. She put the receiver back on the phone and stood there for ten minutes. Then she and Joey sat at the kitchen table. Father had heard the conversation. He had witnessed it. He was too beaten down and resigned to react.

Joey knew his father. He knew what his father had to

have done and gone through before coming home in this condition. He must have argued with the boss. Stood up to him and raised his voice. Argued, not pleaded. His father would not have gotten physical with the boss, but he must have held himself back with enormous effort from beating the living crap out of him.

Twenty minutes. That's all it took. In twenty minutes, Danny was at their door. He took one look at the father and turned to the mother, who was still clutching Joey's hand.

"Tell me."

"Frank's boss on the dock says Frank has no job."

Danny said nothing. He took another look at Joey's father, a man Danny admired because he wasn't a gangster but an honest, hardworking American. Danny left without closing the door behind himself.

Two hours later, with father, mother, and Joey in the kitchen seated at the table, Danny came back. They hadn't closed the front door, so he came right on in and stood in front of the father.

Danny put his massive hand on the father's shoulder and spoke directly to him.

"All is well. No one is taking your job. Go back to the docks tomorrow morning and go to work."

Then Danny turned around and looked at Joey and his mother.

"Don't worry. No one touches my family." Danny smiled and gave a look like an angel looking at the Infant Jesus. He was big and strong. The look he gave was graceful and unforgettable.

He said one more thing. "The boss is gone. He's not coming back." Joey's cousin made him vanish, for good.

Danny left.

The next day, Joey's father came home at the usual time after work. He smiled and kissed his family. From that time forward, Joey was with Danny and worshipped him. Danny didn't replace his parents; no one could take their place. Danny became Joey's hero. A man. He could do no wrong in Joey's eyes, ever. Danny was the one man Joey had to be like.

Cousin Danny introduced Joey to Mr. Carfano and the world in which they both were now integral parts, the Carfano Family. Joey was a bit wild: in fights at Catholic school, punched out a couple of teachers, threw chairs across the lunchroom, things like that. But Joey was intelligent too, and he stood up to bullies. He had both aspirations and desires. School was the streets and his Cousin Danny was the homeroom teacher. Mr. Carfano became Joey's headmaster in crime. Joey served his time in Vietnam in the army as a specialist sharpshooter. He took to guns quickly: a born talent. He was very skilled. Thanks to the army, he was well trained.

Joey inherited his physical features and character from both parents: strength, silent patience, and fortitude from father; fiery black eyes, common wisdom, and compassion for the underdog from mother. From his cousin, he was bequeathed an introduction into the life of organized crime. Consequently, Joey was a rising mob star, home from the war, straight back into the Brooklyn jungle to succeed in the world of men.

In 1971, John Carfano was at the peak of his power and control in Brooklyn. He lost his father at the age of sixteen, in the aftermath of mob revenge that also took out his father's girlfriend, even though the senior Carfano was a made man. The younger Carfano rose steadily through the ranks after serving in the coast guard after World War II and becoming a longshoreman on the Brooklyn docks. A court-ordered psychiatric exam declared him socially unstable or some such nonsense. Like they say, he was crazy as a fox. He earned his loyalty by serving in the Salvucci Family, where he moved up to captain his own crew. His warning to Sallie Dominic of a planned hit made him Dominic's protégé, and eventually he inherited Dominic's Family and was permitted to give it his own name. He was a second-generation Italian-American, with sharp taste in clothes, manners, and a New York accent. Once he stood up to an NYPD detective and said to him, "I'm an American citizen too. I don't have a badge like you."

Because he moved to the head of the line at the relatively young age of forty-one, others envied him and sought, behind his back, to bring him toppling down. Such envy was easy for dumb thugs who lacked the brains to understand that a new generation of gangsters, schooled as Mr. Carfano was by Dominic, and Joey was by Cousin Danny and Mr. Carfano, was the wave of the present.

Now, Joey had a dark sense after their talk, as the Boss put his arms around him. The change in Mr. Carfano wasn't a good one. A thing inside Mr. Carfano had slipped away, deteriorated. Was it his guts or his nerve? Was it his mind? The edge was gone. That edge that put Mr. Carfano ahead of the others, gone. His vision was empty now. Hollow. Joey began to think the Boss saw himself as something or someone he really wasn't cut out to be. This civil rights thing wasn't how a gangster thought out a situation. A public spokesman? No Boss should be that public. A champion for the little man, the Italian little man? That was their customer, who didn't need a champion.

The Italians Joey grew up with and knew wanted a house and a family and a decent job to pay the mortgage and put food on the table. They loved the Catholic Church, their mother, their kids, and their wife, in that order. Next came the USA, the land where a man could make a living. No one Joey knew wanted a champion. Taking some civilian's dollars to join AID was probably a lucrative temporary scam. Making speeches about Italian civil rights was an invitation to disaster.

Joey saw freedom fighters in Vietnam on both sides. They got killed, equally.

Joey could understand the protection racket when your store window was at stake. But he doubted people would keep paying for protecting their heritage. This was not going to end well. This was not a place where Danny, the Boss, and he ought to be.

It was the last week of June, and Joey was preparing to go with Mr. Carfano to the AID rally for "Italians With Pride" at Brooklyn's Grand Army Plaza. Joey told the Boss he was going to bring a piece, but the Boss said don't.

"You stay next to me. If you're pinched with a gun, you're in hot water and I look like I'm corrupting a young man with a valiant military record. I told the Tocca brothers to pack. Besides, the place will be crawling with cops and feds."

If the Boss knew what they really thought about all this, the Toccas would have been the last ones he'd trust to protect him. Joey kept his mouth shut. The Toccas were first, last, and always for themselves. They counted their loyalties in their wallets.

Joey drove the Boss's black Buick Electra 225 Custom Limited, chauffeuring him to the rally. Driving, he asked the Boss where he saw this thing moving to in the future.

"Joey, for once in my life, and I'm in my forties, I see me building a lasting contribution to my heritage. I'm super proud to be an American and to come from Italy. Italians claim Michelangelo, Da Vinci, Columbus, Galileo, and Fermi as ancestors. I see Italians in America electing a president in ten years. You're a young man with the world ahead of you. You're smart and strong. I knew that the first time we met. I want the world to be a better place for you."

"Mr. Carfano, you've already made the world better for me."

"Thanks, Joey. I appreciate that from you. Some of the people around me take what we've built for granted, like it could never end. You and I know better. But there is more to do. I'm a gangster. I'm proud of it. There are lots of Italian-Americans who want nothing to do with us. But they have to have pride too. We can make that happen for them."

He stopped talking and looked out the window as Brooklyn rushed past. He was quiet for two minutes. Then he spoke again.

"I respect Rabbi Kahane. He is a wise man and not afraid to use muscle to defend his people. I am the same."

With that, he didn't say another word until they reached the plaza.

Grand Army Plaza was at the northern corner of Prospect Park, across the way from the Brooklyn Public Library, down Flatbush Avenue. In the plaza was a giant stone arch, honoring the Union soldiers and sailors who fought in the Civil War. It was massive, bigger than the arch in Washington Square Park in Manhattan.

From all directions, on all sides of the plaza, were thousands of people, in a sea of the Italian colors, green, white, and red. Green for the hills and plains. White for the snow-capped Alps. Red for the Italian blood spilled during wars. It was thrilling to see so many people coming together to celebrate their heritage. Joey considered that it might be a good thing to do, after all. He was proud.

Mr. Carfano waded into the crowd. Joey positioned himself to the Boss's right, from behind. Joey concentrated on what and who he could see two steps around them. Who looked or acted out of place? Who wouldn't return Joey's brief stare with a stare? Who was close and why? There were TV cameras and reporters. They wore press badges issued by AID on green, white, and red lanyards around their necks. They were checked before being given permission and access.

About five yards into the crowd, thirty or so feet from the stage under the arch, Joey noticed a tall, well-built black woman, shapely and showing it. She had glossy hair, past her shoulders, and full lips. Very sexy. With her was one of the Tocca brothers, Bobby. Joey knew him too well. Joey didn't like him. Bobby Tocca was a thief and a liar. What was odd about this situation was Bobby was smiling and talking with this black chick. If you knew Bobby Tocca for five minutes, you knew the next word out of his mouth was *moulinyan*, Italian for eggplant, meaning black, but very racist. "F'ing *moulinyan*" this and "f'ing *moulinyans*" that. "The *moulinyans* are apes." "The *moulinyans* are lazy." Bobby once looked out the window of their social club and announced, "There's a load of coal at the door."

Bobby was an asshole about color. The color Joey respected was green, no matter who had it.

Why was he making nice with this black woman? He wouldn't be caught dead talking to a black person.

Standing with her was a black dude who did not fit in the picture. She was sexy, he was scuzzy. She looked like she slept at the Waldorf, on somebody else's dollar. He looked like he woke up in an alley. His clothes were wrinkled and his hair was uncombed. Both of them were wearing press badges.

But something was out of place.

Joey's thoughts went back in Vietnam, and he was picturing in his head another GI. Around the soldier's neck was a dog tag.

What was missing?

The chain. That metal bead chain that held the dog tag.

All the AID press badges were hung on the green-white-red lanyards. Even the black woman's.

The black guy's was hung on a dog tag chain.

Why? Joey's head throbbed. This was all wrong.

The black woman walked over to Mr. Carfano and said, "Hiya, Joe!"

He turned to the sound of her voice. Someone bumped Joey and he lost his balance. It was maybe two seconds later when Joey struggled to get right side up again. He heard three muffled shots. He regained his balance, standing in time to see Mr. Carfano spin backward and land face up on the ground, blood gushing from his mouth and nose. His eyes were fixed upward, and there were bloody air bubbles on his lips. Two yards away, six or seven men were on top of one another, with that black guy's legs sticking out from under the pile. There were four more shots in quick succession and the pile on the ground cleared away, leaving the black guy on his back, lifeless, and bleeding from his chest and forehead. They should have left him alive to tell his story, to say who wanted the Boss dead. Certainly not this black guy by himself. A hit on a boss occurs when everybody agrees.

Joey bent as quickly as he could to Mr. Carfano but something inside him asked, *Who bumped you?* He looked behind. There were dozens of people, though most of the crowd was running in the opposite direction.

One person still standing four yards away from where Joey kneeled and Mr. Carfano lay was Bobby Tocca. Joey caught his eye and Bobby caught his. They stared at each other.

Joey looked away and there was no sign of the black woman.

Spirito.

Like a spirit she had disappeared. No one ever found or named her. Even the chief of the NYPD detectives couldn't find her. She played her part well.

Joey looked at Mr. Carfano on the ground.

He was still breathing, pushing these bloody bubbles out of this mouth and nose. Joey bent down and tried to cradle his head, thinking it would help him breathe. Joey's right hand discovered a bullet hole in the back of the Boss's head.

In what seemed like minutes but were really seconds, two men ran toward Joey, knelt down beside him, and began checking Mr. Carfano's pulse and listening to his respiration.

They were both wearing unpressed black pants and white shirts open at the neck, and yarmulkes. They were followers of Rabbi Kahane, there to support the rally.

One looked at Joey and said firmly, "Leave him be on the ground. We're doctors, we'll take care of him."

Joey looked up at them. Two Jews tending to a fallen Roman warrior.

There were approaching sirens. Three men, dressed similar to the two doctors but with red armbands and stethoscopes, carried a stretcher and set it next to Mr. Carfano. Joey learned later they were members of an Orthodox Jewish volunteer ambulance corps on Flatbush Avenue who were in the neighborhood. The five Jews placed Mr. Carfano on the stretcher and loaded him into their ambulance. Joey's Cousin Danny jumped into the back. The Jews looked at him, decided he was not to be messed with, closed the doors, and took off for the nearest emergency room, which was at Long Island College Hospital in Brooklyn Heights. Joey thanked God that the Boss wasn't being dumped at Brooklyn Hospital close by, which even then was no better than an anteroom for the morgue, even for those not about to die.

A voice over the microphone from the rally stage was telling the crowd not to panic, that the gathering would continue. Joey heard the Ghetto Priest, Father Dennis from the South Bronx, calling the crowd to prayer. His practiced voice echoed off the walls of the arch and the concrete sidewalks. His words touched no one.

No one was paying any attention. Cops were wandering among the crowd, looking like they didn't know what to do. Because they didn't. This was a Family problem, not a public crime. The cops wanted no part in it, and the Family wanted no part of the cops. Everyone kept a distance. It was respect and fear that motivated both sides.

The crowd dispersed as the ambulance took off for the hospital. Joey walked back to Mr. Carfano's car numbly and sat in the driver's seat for an hour, gazing out at the graceful ribbon of Flatbush Avenue, straight ahead through downtown and the shopping district, through the Heights, on to the bridge to Manhattan. He stared at his hands and realized they were covered in drying blood. The Boss's blood. Joey had cradled his head before the Jewish doctors arrived. There was more than blood – there were splotches of pink, chunks of grayish-pink clinging to Joey's shirt cuffs. He thought for a moment. This . . . this hamburger meat was bits of the Boss's scalp and skull and brain that had leaked out. Joey made no attempt to wipe it off. His leader, the man he looked up to, was gone. Joey didn't cry. He didn't want to cry. Women cried, while men planned. What he felt was overwhelming anger that burned hotter than any he had ever experienced or known. He bottled that anger to focus on what had happened. This was not the time for impulse. His vengeance was under restraint so he could calculate when and how to unleash it.

Joey knew that Bobby Tocca was guilty. Joey would do what Mr. Carfano and Cousin Danny had taught him to do. Be patient for revenge. His cousin once told him, "When you want to kill someone, time is your ally. Never let your target know you're going to kill him, and don't rush. Time is in your hands. He dies when you decide. He doesn't know when or who or how. You do." Joey would wait. What counted is what you did, not what you thought about doing. Joey was a man in this world. His cousin instructed him, "Never tell people what you are going to do. Plan it out carefully, then do it." That was what a man did.

The front page of the *Daily News* the next day was a

photo of Mr. Carfano on the stretcher, being lifted into the ambulance. Square-center in the picture was Bobby Tocca, with a cigar stub in his lips, leering at the Boss's body like he was watching a woman undress. Proof enough to Joey of Bobby's guilt.

Mr. Carfano lingered in a coma for seven years, during which his days and nights were filled with terrifying nightmares he was unable to understand, except for the raw torment and fear he felt half awake, half dead, and fully paralyzed, wavering in agony between two worlds. His misery on earth ended in 1978. He met his killer, and those behind his murder, in another place.

To this day, that shooting has never been solved officially. The gunman, Jerome Jones, was a mystery from the fringe of society. No one claimed his body. The police couldn't connect him with anyone. Bobby Tocca blew his own brains out before Joey had the chance. Death took its own time and got payback. Like everybody else, killers don't come out even in the end.

CHAPTER SIX

Ass Bet

Bedford-Stuyvesant, Brooklyn, April 17, 1966

It is always hard to see the purpose in wilderness wanderings until after they are over.
John Bunyan

I was eleven. A tough eleven. I was much stronger physically than most kids my age. I guess I had quality genes. My grandparents, both of them on both sides, were still alive and well into their eighties. I was an ox at eleven, the great-grandson of former slaves.

My parents owned a house on Halsey Street, between Stuyvesant and Reid Avenues, down the block and around the corner, by a few blocks, from where I went to Stephen Decatur Junior High School Number 35. I lived in a white stone rowhouse with three floors and a dirt basement.

The lasting memory I have about that house was a recurring nightmare that kept coming back for four years of tortured sleep. I would be walking up the three flights of stairs from the ground floor to the parlor floor to the top floor; when I reached the bottom step of the last staircase above me, hovering at the head of the stairs was a figure cloaked in black, and although I ran back down away from it, it would remain three steps behind me. I would be wrenched awake, short of breath and sweating, before it caught me. I must have dreamt that once a week for four years.

In my neighborhood, I fell in with the boys who were like me: tough, ambitious, or as ambitious as an eleven-year-old boy could be, and a bit impulsive. My temper would get the best of me at times. I never hurt anyone smaller than me, and I hated anyone who did. I believed in being fair.

A little girl down the block died from the flu. Her open casket was laid out in the living room of her house. Those old rowhouses had indents in the curves of the walls next to the stairs so coffins could make the turns going up and down – the coffin corner. The dead were laid out at home. I was told by my grandmother to go there to pay my respects. The girl's mother greeted me at the parlor floor door and led me to see my dead friend. In an instant, before I could react, the mother took my hand and placed it on the corpse's bare arm. It was marble hard, cold and smooth. I ran from that house back to my home and collapsed on my bed. I had the death dream again that night.

In the street, I became skilled at pitching pennies (or dimes or nickels) just so. Boosting all sorts of stuff from the neighborhood stores, and not getting caught, was another talent I gained from the street academy. Most of what I took I didn't need. It was the thrill that counted. I wouldn't call what I did shoplifting. It was out-and-out theft, and I became very good at it.

Gambling seemed harmless to me as a young man, or

at least victimless. The loser knows what he is going into at the start. Gamblers are willing participants. Either you win or you lose, like life itself. When there was money on the line, tempers might flare up but be expressed in words. I appreciated the energy in gambling, anticipating the roll of the dice or the flip of the cards, risking something for the chance at more. To me, it was a lot like stealing. A big high without drugs and certainly not so dangerous.

At twelve, I rethought this. Saturday nights, me and a group of boys from several blocks around met in a quiet, out-of-the-way basement on McDonough Street. I don't remember who found the spot. It was perfect. A clean stone basement in an old apartment building with storefronts on the ground floor. In the evenings, the stores were closed and no one was the wiser about six teenagers gathered in a basement with a smooth concrete floor. It even had a toilet and sink in a small closet. It was made for our craps games.

There was a Saturday night in late April. The weather was not too hot. To my parents, I was off playing basketball at the schoolyard. My fellow gamblers started shooting and laying down their money. Two older boys in the group were unusually into gambling that night. They were both working after school and earning steady money. Shooting dice was their release.

We began playing, the dice moving around the circle when the shooters couldn't make their number. One of the working boys, Ricky, took his turn and it was his night. He kept making the throws that triggered bigger and bigger bets on him. Ricky's cash was piling up. The other boy, Santo, began to taunt Ricky, yelling "Lose!" at each throw. Ricky seemed to ignore it; he kept the dice and made good on his throws. Finally, Santo blurted out, "Twenty bucks you don't make it!" Ricky took it in stride. After throwing a four, he looked at Santo and calmly threw another four.

We all stood still and quiet.

Ricky told Santo, "Pay up." His voice wasn't angry, he didn't look upset. Not even agitated. It was matter-of-fact.

Santo replied, "No, I'm not paying."

There was an instinct inside me. I moved closer to Ricky, to his right side. I didn't know why, but I knew I was going to be part of something at that moment. Fate was whispering in my ear, and I was listening.

"Ass bet," Ricky said. An ass bet in craps is when you don't have the money but you bet against the shooter anyway. You lose, you can't pay up. It's a dumb play with no percentage.

"Screw your ass bet, Ricky. I ain't paying."

"You ain't got it? Ass bet me?" Ricky moved an inch or two nearer to Santo. I was at Ricky's side.

I was a half step behind Ricky's movement when he produced a knife from his right pants pocket, flipped the blade open, and lunged at Santo's neck. I caught Ricky's arm as it flew across Santo's face. He actually nicked Santo's throat, a bare touch that drew blood from the skin. I forced Ricky's right arm back and down. My grip latched on and it was steel. His knife arm was immobilized and wouldn't move until I let it. Ricky didn't resist; he went limp.

Santo stood there stunned. He'd overplayed his hand. He never imagined Ricky was packing a blade and would get to the breaking point. Santo didn't touch his neck wound. The trickle of blood ran onto the collar of his white T-shirt. It wasn't a deep cut, probably didn't hurt much.

The suddenness was terrifying. Santo could have been dead in a flick of that blade, and he knew it.

I was concentrating on Ricky. Although he looked calm seconds before, now he was trembling.

He started muttering to himself. Standing next to him I made out what he was saying. "I could have died. I could have died. If I killed him, I could have died. Over dice. Over dice. I could have died."

Ricky dropped the knife. I let go of his arm. He picked up his money from the floor, looked down at the dice and spat, then walked away. He was gone.

As far as I know, Ricky never shot craps with the group again. Maybe he saw his future staring back at him in those dice? The eyes of death. Ricky saw death in a flash – what could have been became real, as real as what did and didn't happen. Both realities were possible in a split second.

We grab at death daily and don't see it until later. We dodge traffic crossing the street. We catch ourselves falling asleep at the car wheel. Death taps us on the shoulder, but we ignore it. Death is the most diligent worker. Death doesn't retire or take a day from the office. Death doesn't get sick. Death doesn't age. Death doesn't quit. We do.

After that dice game, I knew death was pursuing me in my dreams – I got a glimpse of him in that basement and now could feel how close he was behind me everywhere. Interestingly enough, it wasn't death that made me stop and think. It was the suddenness of it all or, rather, the fact that I couldn't see it until afterward. Life wasn't worth it if I spent my time, even some of my time, looking behind at that spook at the top of the stairs. I wasn't going to go forward if I was glancing backward. No, I had to commit to moving forward. I couldn't see an alternative. I wasn't a quitter.

I developed an attitude from that incident to now: I let go of fear. Fear was useless. Living in fear meant dying a coward. The opposite of fear was faith. I had to have faith in something, in myself. Mostly, that became knowing who I was, where I was, and what I was doing. Life wasn't careless and I wouldn't be either. Whenever I was challenged in a situation, I would repeat, "It's up to me." I learned to rely on myself – I was my responsibility, and if I foolishly turned that responsibility over to others, I was begging to be hurt. Death was the big, bad wolf if I let it haunt me. No way.

I didn't have that death dream again. There was no more fear.

That was my confirmation at twelve. I was young, but I wised up early. Catholic kids I knew got confirmed in their midteens, in church. I got confirmed in that basement at twelve. Some people don't make it that far. Some never get there. They spend their lives afraid of their possibilities and stay married to fear forever. That wasn't for me.

CHAPTER SEVEN

On the Mountaintop

Financial District, Manhattan, Spring 1999

The devil's finest trick is to persuade you
that he does not exist.
Charles Baudelaire

I didn't know what it was when I first met her.

She had coal-black eyes and a full mane of thick black hair streaked with auburn highlights that would make a lioness envious. Her nose was a remnant of Mediterranean heritage, neither pointed nor flat but prominent and very attractive. Her body was by no means skinny; she was full, not fat, with curvy legs and nicely tapered ankles. From a rearview, you knew she was a she. And her cheekbones were high and pinkish-tan.

She was Jewish and plenty sharp. When she spoke, both her words and her face held your attention, especially those big dark eyes.

I had no notion of what lurked inside her, but she made me want to learn. We were sitting in a restaurant awaiting dinner and she said to me, "Which do you want more, this food or me? I have the key to a hotel room.

Who'll give you a better offer?" What questions! Did I live by food alone? At that moment she was temptation pure and direct. We skipped dinner.

I thought I knew her, understood her. I deceived myself that I did. I didn't know it. Her allure was so powerful that I made myself absolutely believe everything she said and did. I thought I knew it. She didn't offer me an apple to eat. She gave herself.

We were standing at the window of the Millennium Hotel, across from the World Trade Center, looking out from the twenty-fifth floor after an entire morning of lovemaking, and she asked me, "If you threw yourself out this window, do you believe I would catch you?" Those eyes were piercing my body, and my head was spinning as if we both actually threw ourselves from that window while we were in the hotel's bed and were descending at gathering speed, entwined into the bottomless pit of our shared lust. And I believed her. I believed it. We returned to that bed and made more love.

In the fall and winter of nineteen years ago, we met at work and rapidly developed a close friendship. No more than two weeks into it, we were lunching together every workday. We formed our own two-person clique at the office. Nominally, I was her manager and she was the head of her own department. Practically, once our relationship deepened and intensified, she was managing me and I hadn't even noticed the change. Though others quarreled with her and denounced her, I stood up for her. I bore the arrows meant for her, until I became the target because of her. I took it all unquestioningly. It was my cause. It was what mattered. It was my life.

It was as natural and evolutionary as a newborn baby

suckling its mother. That's what I came to be in short order, the baby at his mother's breast: connected, dependent, inseparable. I loved that sweet, nourishing breast. I returned to that place from where I first arrived. I was her defense and she laughed at those attacking her. Her baby wouldn't betray her. She was wickedly clever, more so than me.

"This is all yours. Forever." She stood in front of me in her skin. It was lovely, accommodating skin. All I could see was perfection. She was the world, and it was mine at that instant. I took it voraciously and begged for more.

Three temptations, out of thousands of temptations. She played them and I grabbed for the line, oblivious to the barbed hook that it stuck in my throat. I was deaf and blind. I heard and saw nothing, most of all nothing in myself. I allowed it complete control – no, not allowed; I granted it that, willingly. There was no more me but me inside it and it inside me. My body and soul and all, they were hers.

Forever was five years. Not a lot of time. She saw the chance to move on and hunt elsewhere. It started to fade. In small ways at first. Missed dinners where she directed me to one place but called to see why I wasn't there at another. Gaslight – like in the film. She caressed another man's face in front of me, smiling at me to say, *See, I can hook someone else before your eyes, but you won't even trust what you see. Even as I disengage from you, expel you from my warmth and my body, leave you without giving any reason or notice, kiss you one day and spurn your kiss the next, you'll still believe in it. It has owned your soul. Now, it sinks its teeth into someone new. A fresh victim. New flesh. Hotter passion. Desperation.* She telephoned me and had the man she was with be heard in the background while she and I spoke. She stopped being available.

This was her new game. She left a card in her car, a card from her new conquest, a card that stated explicitly that she had a new lover, still in addition to her husband: then she asked me to drive her car so I could find it. He was a doctor, unattractive, crippled, and married, the spitting image of a famous TV comedian, but he was also everything she craved – a totally subservient, sightless, helpless worshipper. She seduced him in his treatment room. He believed everything she said. Her enemies became his enemies. He followed faithfully. To tennis at the health club and breakfast hideaways and dark nightclubs, limping behind it, trying to be worthy of it. It was thrilling him. She gave him the bait and hid the hook. He consummated his lust as a beggar at a banquet, drooling like a famished schoolboy over her body.

She was the sovereign of liars. She denied the relationship with him, even in the face of evidence of people seeing and hearing them together intimately. "How could you say that?" It was the master act of a grand illusionist; woo you to your face, cut you up on the side. She continued to live and defy the plain, observed truth. The collateral pain she brought wasn't her concern: her own family, the wife and children of her conquest. No other thing was important – it conquered, that was all.

Unlike other schemers who were eventually laid low by their own works, she prospered from victim to victim. I was told by persons in the know, she called him on a rainy night to be with her in a local motel. Compelled, driven, pulled by desire, he ran. In the parking lot, he stumbled on a curbstone, his bum leg giving out on him, fell, and struck his head. A massive heart attack did the rest. I imagine his mind was so flooded with passion that in his last moment he couldn't distinguish between coming and going.

In response to his death, she brazenly sent a public condolence note to his wife and children, like nothing between her and him occurred, punctuating the evil within it. A week later, she had a new acolyte. The Spanish language has a fit term for it, *sin vergüenza,* without shame. All of this, in front of her family. Too late, I realized that I could have always told when it was a lie – when her lips were moving. It was always a lie, all of it. She spoke her native language, deceit.

We were parted and each year later, in the month of March, around her birthday, she would leave a voicemail or send an e-mail or call my cell to teasingly remind me of what had been. She offered to explain it to me, though we were years apart. "Give me a call. I think of you when I wear the dolphin necklace you gave me." I refused it by staying silent and unresponsive, but I shook in shame remembering my own squalid self-centeredness. I wasn't blameless. I saw in a mirror what I was. I was pulled in by it without resistance. I was a sinner by choice. A free will sinner. I had put my faith in a person, and that misplaced faith was found sadly wanting.

Nineteen years after we first met, in early April, I sorted through my bookshelves, searching for volumes I had forgotten. I found, tucked away, a small book filled with movie stills from slapstick comedy shorts, with captions praising fatherhood. I read it with a relaxed laugh, puzzled at how I had acquired it. I turned to the title page's inscription: "I saw this and had to give it to you. You are a lovable guy. Love ya." The sight of her handwriting emptied my breath. In March one year later, she invaded my dream, her face vivid and her voice as clear as a bell. "You weren't good enough for me," she said. Would I ever be rid of this malignant presence? Can such a pervasive cancer ever be totally removed? What medicine could kill it?

It took several years for me to see it for what It was.

It.

First, on the top of the mountain, It asked, "If you are who they say you are, you can turn these stones into bread and eat."

Then It said, "If you are who they say you are, then fall off this mountain and you will be caught before you are injured."

Finally, It offered, "Everything you see from here is yours if you come to me."

She was It.

I confessed bitterly to a friend, "I slept with Satan." Half of that devil was me.

It invades lives every day. It destroys and laughs. It is the most beautiful thing you can imagine. It can be a man or a woman or anything else It wants to be to you. It transforms Itself at will. It speaks enchanting words. It tempts you to feast on sweet poison. It can make you eat your own excrement, return to your mistakes, and have you kill for more. It is attractive and funny and captivating. It is ubiquitous. It is all you can see. It shines so alluringly. It dazzles. It is roaring, unquenchable fire. We light our fuse for this self-destructive blaze.

Was I fortunate to recognize It before I was burned up

by what It kindled in me? I could have been incinerated and taken others with me. Maybe I did and don't acknowledge it. It left pain and destruction in Its wake. It killed something in me I cannot recover: my trust and part of my soul. What am I capable of doing now for desire? I shudder.

This can be you or not. It enters your life if you let It, but frequently before you know It. It has no innate power of Its own, save your own greed and lust and avarice and weakness, but It uses that which is in you to destroy you from the inside out.

CHAPTER EIGHT

The Real Deal

Bensonhurst, Brooklyn, June 15, 1959

But every man is more than just himself.
Hermann Hesse

The story of New York is most often a story from elsewhere.

Up to the age of ten, I thought I was an Italian. We lived in a neighborhood full of Italians, Bensonhurst, Brooklyn; we went to church and school with other Italians; we ate Italian food always; and my elders spoke Italian among themselves.

Though my parents definitely wanted me to be an American, they lived our lives Italian, nothing else. "Don't play with that boy, his parents aren't one of us." "You go to Mr. Fazio's butcher store, not the Jewish one!" "This is how my grandparents did it back home – good enough for them, good enough for us." "You eat your macaroni. It's good for you." "Marry a good girl (wink, wink), one of ours."

Not that we disliked other people; their way of life just

wasn't for us. I could be anything I wanted to be when I got older, but I would forever be an Italian.

Or so I thought.

At age ten, my father took me aside to give me the facts of life. No, not about the birds and the bees and between a girl's knees. The facts of being Sicilian. He decided it was time. In my day father talked, son listened.

"Now you have to know what you are. We are Sicilians. Let me tell you what that is," he said.

Sicilians are not Italians. They're Sicilians. Italians are foreigners. Their parents weren't born in Sicily and that meant they didn't eat, speak, sleep, talk, walk, live, or see life as Sicilians do. Sicily was different and special. Sicily was better.

"Before 1861 there was no Italy until Garibaldi united it. To Sicilians, he was another invader, taxing our mules, our food, everything. For those in Naples and to the south, nothing changed."

That part of Italy plus Sicily and Sardinia, the *mezzo giorno*, was called "the land forgotten by time." Almost 90 percent of Italians who came here came from that part. Father explained that, unlike other immigrant groups, for Sicilians, there was no great silence after their exodus. His family talked about Sicily and pined for the dream of their homeland once in America. Life in Sicily had been harsh, but their souls and memories never left that place.

"Italy attacked Sicily many times. Those people came for us. They killed Sicilians and robbed us. They tried to conquer us. But – they failed. Sicily remains and Sicilian blood is strong."

Father commented, "To show you what animals the Italian government was, when King Umberto was shot, his assassin was thrown into a four-foot cell, for life! After not much time, he was moved to a mental institution because being crunched drove him insane! Can you imagine such people?"

He went on to give me a history of Sicily. I say "a" history because, to this day, I'm not convinced if his stories were 100 percent the facts. I learned another part of being Sicilian is we're one helluva storyteller. Where the facts are shaky, we fill in the blanks, a lot. You see, a lack of evidence never stops us from telling a story.

Why did my father's people leave Sicily to emigrate to the Golden Land, America? Sicily, a land used to upheaval, revolt, and invasion, became hotter than ever in the 1860s. The city of Palermo revolted against Garibaldi's unification, following Sicily being absorbed into the Kingdom of Italy. Italy responded by bombing Palermo and executing the peasants. The *brigantaggio* started insurrections across the island, and Italy sent troops to suppress them. Most of these brigands were peasants, like my forebearers. They were single-minded, overtaxed, and not the type to be bullied by a distant government. Authority was the enemy. To them, Italy was another country because it wasn't Sicily. My people were fiercely self-reliant. When the economy, which in Sicily was almost completely farming, fell apart, those who could, and even some who really couldn't, left for the promise of America. They believed "he who leaves, survives." That's how my paternal great-grandfather Pasquale came here, after twelve torturous days at sea. My mother's people followed a similar pattern from Naples, after a cholera epidemic in the 1880s and civil uprisings. What my father was, I was – Sicilian.

In the first twenty years of the century, three million

Italians entered America through Ellis Island. Many Sicilians went to New Orleans, part of which became famously nicknamed "Little Palermo." My people stayed in New York.

Coincidentally, when Sicily's economy and independence began collapsing and outside forces, including foreign Italy and France, began intruding, the so-called *mafia* arose. These men were united by the cause of defending Sicilian honor, women, and family. These original *mafiosi* were seen by the natives as the buffer between the people and the government. They were defenders. They were protection. They were Sicily against a hostile and dangerous world. They were, in reality, extortionists, who preyed on their own and made riches while playing the role of Robin Hood. Indeed, they were hoods. So much of Sicily and Italy's history was a story of fighting both outside and internal forces.

I am a descendent of a naturally rebellious race. Everybody from Charles I of France to Napoleon to Garibaldi to Mussolini to Hitler has tried to control us, like some farm animals, and failed. Although we were country people, we wouldn't be corralled like sheep, led to the slaughter like cattle, or made to eat our own droppings like the hens!

My father's words were, "We won't be chained. When threatened, we bare our claws and we don't run. We take kindness and like companions, but we guard what is ours and don't let anyone boss us or our territory. We distrust the stranger, *strániu,* which is what all non-Sicilians are. We are honest, bold, loud, and tough. But you will not find a race of people who are more humble, welcoming, and gentle."

He told me a legend that during the time the French ruled Sicily, almost eight hundred years ago, a young woman was returning home after Mass one Sunday morning. She was accosted by a French soldier who violated her innocence. The locals found out, but most felt powerless in the face of the armed French military occupiers. A courageous band of men vowed to right this monstrous wrong. They waylaid the Frenchman and slit his throat, then displayed his body in the public square. This was followed by a full-scale anti-French riot. Since the French didn't speak or understand Sicilian, whenever a local saw a member of the heroic band of men, the word *mafia* would be whispered – "boldness."

Oddly, if you describe a woman as *mafiusa* in the Sicilian language, that means she is beautiful. In America, the word *mafia* did not come into wide usage until 1890, when the race riot and lynching of eleven Sicilians in New Orleans made it a common term describing all Italians. This was the largest mass lynching in American history. It still is.

My father's father was Tonino, who owned a carpentry shop on Fulton Street in Brooklyn. He inherited his carving skills from generations of woodworkers back home. My father's mother was Nancy Lucini; her cousin was the infamous Lucky Luciano. Grandma Nancy would have nothing to do with gangsters. She detested them and devoted her life in America to her children, grands, and the Church. Grandparents Tony and Nancy lived on Court Street near Hicks Street in South Brooklyn. My grandfather told me his father's nickname was "Tony," even though his given name was Pasquale, because when he came to Ellis Island, the guards stamped "To NY" on his papers! To me growing up, they were loving grandparents.

When he finished his-story, my father recited the names of Sicily's invaders. "Carthaginians, Greeks, Romans, Arabs, Barbarians, Normans, Angevins, Aragonese, Moors, Germans, Italians, British, Americans. Our home has seen all of these in one way or another. Sicily was entered and violated but never enslaved by any of these. We may have a drop of foreign blood but by God we are Sicilians."

He added, "Being here in America was no paradise either. Sicilians were stupid dirt farmers – superstitious and uncouth. The Italians from the north told their American buddies that that was what we were. Sicilians had dark skin, and that was a sign of inferiority in this country, like the blacks. White social workers told my parents that they didn't know how to feed me; bread must be bleached flour, not brown, and breakfast must be oatmeal. You know what oatmeal was to Sicilians? Pig slop. Imagine coming here and being told to give your children pig slop! The Irish ran the Church here, and we were ordered to worship in the basement. In the west, General Dimwit detained ten thousand Italians as possible enemies of the US at the start of the Second World War. Most of them were old people, fishermen, and waiters, who hurt no one. They lost their homes, businesses, liberty, and some committed suicide rather than be caged like beasts, thanks to Roosevelt with his nose stuck up in the air. In New York, the majestic singer Pinza was arrested and jailed without charges because he was an Italian on contract to the Metropolitan Opera. We had to endure this, but we survived and remained Sicilian. With all that, Americans were ten times better than Garibaldi and his gang."

Two years later, when I was twelve, my father introduced me to his cousin Domenico Greco, who came from Sicily to visit us in Brooklyn. The evening he arrived, my mother prepared a feast of Sicilian specialties: *arancini* (fried rice balls filled with cheese), lentil soup, *pasta con le sarde* (bucatini pasta and fresh sardines), *involtini* (veal rolls with tomatoes, raisins, and pine nuts), and *bianco-mangiare* (almond milk custard) for dessert.

After dinner we all sat in the living room, the old folks drinking their *anisette* and me enjoying a treat of watered-down sweet wine in a small tumbler. Cousin Domenico was encouraged to tell me his life story.

"I was born near Mount Etna in 1898." Looking at him, I would have guessed he was in his forties – no paunch; full, unlined face; big nose; a head of mostly jet-black curly hair; and steel-gray eyes. His back was ramrod straight. His features proved his last name, "Greek" in Italian, was well earned.

"When I was young, my birthplace was called Castro-giovanni, the Fort of John, before Il Duce changed it. My uncles toiled in the sulfur mines owned by Napoleone Colajanni. For a brief time then, Sicily was prosperous for more than farming. That didn't last."

He paused and rubbed his head with his big, rough hand.

"My father was a barber and so I was one too. I was too young to fight in the first war and too hidden from the government to be drafted by Il Duce. But come 1939, somehow my reputation barbering got back to Rome.

"I cut hair and shaved faces. I was a good barber. I mended the miners' broken hands and arms. I taped cuts.

Somehow, Il Duce learned how good I was. I was summoned to Rome and presented before him. He looked me over, in his grand office, and told me, 'From now on, you live here. Each morning you give me a shave. My people tell me you can shave a balloon with a straight razor and not make it pop.' I look at him and say, 'Yes, sir.' 'Good,' he tells me. I get whisked away. I have my own apartment near his palace. Good food. A fancy uniform. Nice pay. I'm over the moon. This is the way to spend a war.

"Good times never last long. The war starts to go badly. Some government flunky calls me one day and says, 'You going to war. Get over to the military headquarters.' I go and off I am for Sardinia. The Thirtieth Infantry, Sabauda." He pointed to a faded green military patch with a gold sword and oak clusters stitched on his sweater. "One month I'm there and a corporal finds me in a tent in the countryside and says, 'What the hell you doing here? Il Duce needs a shave!' They were looking for me. Government workers! One hand is scratching the ass, the other is picking the nose. Back I go to Rome and keep shaving his head. Not too long, the war is lost. Il Duce's aide tells me, 'Ditch your uniform and dress like a farmer and get the hell out of here.'

"I follow his advice and hook up with two others, one a fellow." Domenico put his forefinger to the side of his nose. This meant the fellow was *mafia*.

"The three of us walk from Rome to the Strait of Messina," the channel between the toe of the boot and Sicily, "and we look for a boat to get across. We have no money. We've been living off strangers, stealing and hunting. I will never take another bite of rabbit for the rest of my life! We get water where we find it and relieve ourselves in the woods, with leaves to wipe. This fellow, he tells us two, he has a plan. He talks a fisherman into rowing us across the strait, then he robs him. We're back in Sicily.

"We break up, each going to his hometown. Later I hear this fellow was shot dead after robbing the wrong farmer. I get back there, but I don't want to stay. It takes time. I borrow some money from an uncle and get a ship to America. I end up here in Brooklyn with a cousin, Giorgio on Baltic Street, and I start barbering. Giorgio is an animal, but I make an honest dollar. A couple of years, I have my own shop. Pretty good. Nice living. When I was a little boy, I was told the very air in America killed the Italian family. Not so: I meet Rosa, a Calabrese girl, and we marry. Wonderful years. Good life doesn't go forever. Rosa dies, no children. I'm alone again. I want back to Sicily. I sell everything I own, my house and shop, and I come back. Then, after the war and the Americans, Sicily changed. The candy factories turn into heroin mills. First, Genovese runs them, then Luciano takes them over. The sulfur mines are tapped out. Farmers eat grass. The drug business makes the money. I stay alive. Now I'm there, six years. I look up at the mountain and tend my fruit trees and think about Rosa. Good times never last long."

Am I truly more Sicilian than Italian? I still don't know. Listening to Cousin Domenico, I saw in him a sort of submission to the inevitable that my parents also exhibited. "Good times never last long." Conversely, they were tenacious against life's day-to-day trials, and they taught me to fight if I believed I was in the right. Some days you catch the bear, other days he catches you. Don't give up or in. America, for most immigrants and surely for my family, has been both a blessing and a curse. I was told to stand my ground and fight, and I did.

The more I learn about my father's homeland and its people, a sturdy bunch who overcame a relentless tide of bad fortune, the more I see of them in me. They persist.

I am an American with the lifelines of Sicily in my soul. In this country, the memory of Sicily is probably more powerful and beautiful than the reality.

CHAPTER NINE

The Lesson of One Day

East Tremont, The Bronx, August 6, 1965

Hell is other people.
Jean Paul Sartre

Arthur

One more day. I say that each and every miserable morning. One day today and one day tomorrow. If they aren't all exactly the same, they produce the same misery, one after one, after one. I'm awake and in the same place, like a walking, breathing form of sleep paralysis.

A twelve-year-old boy I met at the park, tried to explain to me what sleep paralysis was. How this urchin ever learned this term was itself a great mystery and amusement. I suspect his father was a doctor; there are loads of them in my neighborhood. I hadn't known the term until a couple of years ago, and I had it explained to me by my younger brother. It is the agony of struggling to breathe on the verge of wakefulness, the body unresponsive to the brain caught in the throes of trying to get itself

75

awake. It's a terror, a body-wracking battle of fighting inside to climb outside of sleep.

The twelve-year-old said it was a monster, some kind of dragon, pulling a person into death, and the person was fighting against it.

The boy was more poetic than my brother, though both of them were correct. It happened to me occasionally when I went to sleep dehydrated or neglected to floss and brush my teeth, the residue of undigested sugar in my mouth leaving me parched and breathing through my mouth instead of my nose, drying me out. Or my bedroom wasn't sufficiently ventilated during a dry night's sleep. I'm sure if I shed about thirty pounds, that would help as well. Whatever – I hate those paralytic seconds of gasping, pulling myself out of sleep.

Almost as much as I hate my life awake, struggling to be set free of the prison in which I'm sentenced to live, for life. My life as an office worker, a junior-level accountant in a big law firm, surrounded by people half my age who make ten times my salary. My life as a New Yorker, enduring dirty streets, stinking air, off-tasting water, thugs and beggars, shrieking kids, and loudmouthed adults. The buses, cars, and subways. The shoulder-to-shoulder, crotch-to-crotch, smelly bipeds walking over me, standing so close I know what they ate for breakfast. The entire rotten, unwashed bunch.

If I were fortunate, fortunate in my life I'm saying, my home would be a resort from this, but it isn't. I live where I can barely afford to, where my wife and I can barely afford to. It's an old, gray apartment building in a once fine neighborhood, filled with several couples like us and doctors and dentists.

I didn't have it to become a doctor. Despite my parents nagging me as a kid, I studied numbers, for what it's worth. I saw my dad work himself to exhaustion during the Great Depression, making a living doing house calls and medicating our neighbors on suicide watch. I wasn't going to be a doctor. Accountants looked at papers, not tragedies.

Then there's my wife. Betty. For the last ten years. Make that an even, round century, because every year with her is ten years' worth of pain. I don't hate her – I hate what she is. She's the same as when we first met, only more so. Those things about her that were at first minor annoyances – her tics and mannerisms, her off-kilter views of the world and other people – have blossomed into an unbearable, unlivable alien with which I reside in an extremely close space called marriage.

You cannot understand hoping at night, praying that in the morning she'll go to work and at noon, I'll receive a telephone call, "Sorry to have to give you this news, but your wife was struck and killed by a truck." I'm fantasizing that the truck is a Marlboro delivery van, for the candy-coated justice that she quit smoking five years ago. And it has malfunctioning brakes so that the driver is innocent of responsibility. I don't want her demise to be on anyone's hands but on circumstance. Pure bad, blind happenstance.

Divorce her? Why carry all this anger on my conscience when a quickie divorce could set me free? I don't have the will or the dough. After a divorce, she'd still be breathing, sharing the same air as me, strolling about as obnoxious as ever. Not with me, of course, but alive to poison the atmosphere with her judgmental negativity, and me out several thousand bucks from my pocket. The possibility would exist that she could have a mind to call me or write, and my torment wouldn't be ended for good. No, no. If I'm going to hope, I'm hoping for a complete end, good and final. And cost-free.

For the last five years, I've armed myself with a strategy; maybe not the best strategy, but one that's worked. I listen to her with a small smile, nodding intermittently to signal I'm paying attention, and patiently assenting, "Yes, you're right" and "Uh-huh." That's enough to keep her going, talking utter nonsense, manufacturing facts as she prattles, reading everyone's mind, and passing omniscient judgment on all situations. Additionally, I mustn't forget her being a victim. The constant victim, the recipient of the world's ill will. Oh, the crosses she builds and then hangs herself on could, deconstructed and rearranged, erect a landmark skyscraper.

Coupled with hoping she dies the next day, this is my strategy for living in a home with her. Thank goodness we don't have offspring. I would have taken my own life by now. I would have looked in the mirror in the morning and have had to decide whether to slit her throat or my own. When told by Nancy Astor that if he were her husband, she would poison his tea, Churchill replied, "If I were your husband, I'd drink it." That would have been me, had I procreated with my wife. Thanks for small favors.

Just plain tell her I can't stand her? I don't have the guts to kick over the whole apple cart. Ten years means being crippled, with nowhere else to go.

I read a book and one of the characters said, "Marry and be damned!" I did.

There is no self-pity in me. I made my bed. I am not the forty-year-old man who outlived my future by twenty years and my past by another twenty. I am neither wicked and moral nor good and immoral. That's Churchill speaking again. I'm in my own fix and only my own departure will relieve me. There are mornings I wish I hadn't survived the night.

I do go on, don't I?

Telling my story is an inadequate safety valve to let out steam before my internal boiler explodes. Nevertheless, I'm grateful for the opportunity.

Betty

He's just cranky. I don't have to be told what he's said. Don't tell me, please. I know him. Boy, do I know him. After eleven years, I know him well. He's okay – acts sullen more than is justified by the smooth little life he enjoys, getting his way all the time, but I'm okay with it. He's faithful, never went off the reservation, I made sure of that. The number of times I've accused him and been in his face, he's never stepped out on me. Probably he had the urge like most fellas, could be he's taken one to lunch, and that's it. He's stuck to our vows and so have I.

After eleven years with him, what good would fooling around do for me; tell me, what good? A roll in the hay? For what? I'd always come home, just like my husband. He comes home every evening because he doesn't have time to go catting. I have his hot tea, in a water glass with a spoon and three heaps of sugar stirred in. I'm into my second gin on ice with a lemon wedge, and we sit in the living room, telling each other about the day. My work, his work. He's enjoying his tea, so not much to report from him. He listens and that's his good point – he's a listener. I can tell him everything, anything, and he listens with a smile. I do appreciate that in him.

I sell dresses at S. Klein on the Square, on Fourteenth Street in the city. It's a living, barely, but it's work. When I come home, I want a gin on the rocks and my hubby's ear. I get both. I'm a happy girl. A guy is entitled to be cranky now and then. I feel for him. I make the tea to soothe him. He's a good guy. An honest, one-of-a-kind breadwinner; not a doctor like his father, but he's my breadwinner, thank heavens. Wife of a doctor would have been nice. I guess it wasn't in the cards. What matters is he brings home his pay. He's steady, reliable like a brick.

We've lived here in East Tremont since our wedding; actually, since before we got married. Our parents lived in this building, and both of our fathers were doctors who also had offices here. This apartment was his family's. He inherited it from them when they passed in '62, and we just moved in – not such a big step for us, because we lived with my folks two floors above after we married. This is Mount Hope Court, once the tallest building in the Bronx and still a known address. Seven large rooms, big kitchen, formal dining room, eight closets! As you can see, the building is shaped like a wedge. It looks like the little brother of the Flatiron Building, fitting in snugly on the corner of a triangle block. It's our little love nest.

We're neighborhood kids, natives of the area. We played and petted in Echo Park. You need to see Echo Park. That's not the official name, but us neighborhood kids called it that due to the echoes bouncing off the rocks and cliffs cut by the Ice Age. The boulders moved across the land, and some got stuck here. Echo Park – we have lasting memories of Echo Park. Him and me kissing at dusk and other romantic things we did there. We share our lives in this place, in this building.

You know, this East Tremont used to be owned by a tobacco millionaire family, the Lorillards. To show you how loving my husband is, about six years ago he said, "Quit smoking, it'll kill you. You've been at it since you're a teenager. Take care of yourself, for goodness' sake. Don't you want to live?" Well, I hadn't seen it that way, you know, killing myself, but he made sense. Smoking was like rolling a dollar bill and setting it on fire. I quit like that, cold, overnight. One week later and I'm cigarette-free ever since. Thanks to my husband, bless his heart.

We're hooked, see? Hooked together like a pattern in lace; we can't be unraveled or picked apart. His life is my life and mine is his. Our parents were friends. We were friends. Then we were lovers. Now husband and wife.

He has his moods, though I can't say he's a moody person. We all have our moods. He's a good man, decent and loyal. I count on him. He'll never leave, and we'll never leave our home.

I know people. A lot of them are miserable. They're lonely, even the married ones, just plain lonely and bitter. A lot are jealous; some of them jealous of me and what I have. Wouldn't some of them love to be married to my husband? I know people, and they can be stubborn and hard to please. My hubby is a rock. I know how to keep him happy and at home. He knows what he's got.

I couldn't live without him. There wouldn't be anything to live for without him. He is my memories, my life. I'm not someone alone. I can't be alone, but I don't know what I'd do if he died first. Oh my God, I don't want to think about it. Why live if half your life is in the grave? Tell me, why live? Maybe, I'll walk over to the zoo and jump in the lion cage!

Look – I don't mean to rush you out, but here's your hat, what's your hurry? Gotcha! I'm not being rude. He'll be home soon, and I haven't had my first gin on the rocks and I haven't started his tea. I'd ask you to stay and break bread, but it's Friday. We're calling Chicken Delight and watching Uncle Walter on channel 2.

Nice talking to you. My husband and I are happy and in love. Understand?

His job at the law firm continued for another nine years, and he and his wife needed it because S. Klein closed, and she had to take a cashier's position at a local discount store in the Bronx Hub, a deteriorating central business district in the Melrose section. Simultaneously with that neighborhood's decline, East Tremont started a backward slide as the entrenched middle- and working- classes felt pressured to move north, first to other sections of the borough and onward to Yonkers, due to poorer citizens fleeing urban desolation in the South Bronx and massive urban renewal developments.

Where husband and wife felt safe and secure now morphed into a sketchy neighborhood, with increased crime, grime, and neglect. For their vastly different motivations, they remained together until a day in 1975 when he was struck and killed crossing the treacherous intersection of Willis, Third, and Melrose Avenues, going to see his wife. He was hit by a Garment District truck bringing factory seconds to a bargain store in the Hub named Spark's – Where Easy Credit is King, down the block from his wife's employer. The driver swore the man looked him dead in the eye and continued walking deliberately in front of the truck, without any terror on his face. The wife arrived at the scene, out of unknowing curiosity, to find her husband already covered with a white sheet.

Her grief drowned her in gin on the rocks. One month later, she swallowed five Nembutals and washed them down with her favorite drink. The Nembutals were prescribed to help her sleep after the trauma of her husband's death. By the time of her death, her only survivors were cousins, who buried her without knowing much about her life. No one, other than her husband, knew much about her life.

Her resting place is next to her husband's in Saint Raymond's Cemetery on Balcom Avenue, not to be confused with New Saint Raymond's Cemetery, though both are east of the Hutchinson River Parkway. Their mutual plot is within walking distance of thousands of other final resting places of the famous and the unheralded.

What this husband and wife had in common in their life was their unlearned lesson that the stability of their souls, their internal environment, the milieu interieur, is the key to a healthy physical and spiritual life, and to happiness. What's inside is independent of what's on the outside, and it is capable of conquering external elements. In a way, living is like focusing an internal camera. When the focus is widened, the light is dispersed, and so is the individual clarity. But, when the focus is narrowed, the light is intensified. The resolution of the subject becomes clearer.

Thus, their stories here are now done.

CHAPTER TEN

Last Dance

Jackson Heights, Queens, March 11, 1961

One is truly dead only when one is no longer loved.
Théophile Gautier

The time came and he was gone. He died – not alone – in his own bed, and she was with him. It came: at first, she didn't notice. He was comfortable. He didn't rattle or cough; it was nothing like the movies, no violent thrashing or moaning, no seeing a light and calling out, *I'm going.* Nothing like that at all, and after her wondering, *Is this the end? What should I do? Do I prepare?* No, she did not have to do anything except look at him in peace and give thanks that so gentle a life had ended gently.

She knew it was coming, as it had been for months now. His quiet heart unwinding after over sixty years with her, failing at last with so much wear and use, a fine-tuned instrument reaching its capacity and slowly, gradually coming to a stop. She suspected that would be it; in fact, she prayed the inevitable would be this graceful, just as he had been. Heroic and kind to him and to her.

For months, her questions were not how, but when; not why, but why not.

Now, maybe she wanted to go too, though that would not be by her own hand, because his death would not be answered by her to cause another death. If her heart was broken, and, after these warm years it was, her soul was intact, and it was a soul that couldn't take a life, not even her own. Perhaps there wasn't a great deal to live for now. There was enough inside her to go on living, not for his memory, but for herself.

She had always been quicker witted, the wiser one. He was the softer one, full of spirit and generous in understanding, especially patiently understanding her. They both learned to forgive each other quickly, whether for real or imagined faults. This was their love.

A month ago, they sat listening to a song, all the while knowing silently that his will was submitting to his last journey here. They cast that aside for an evening together, holding hands and getting up to dance in each other's arms. The song was sung by Sinatra.

They're impatient for us to go home. We can't pull ourselves apart. Eventually we will, but not right now.

They held each other for the eternity of several minutes and sat holding hands once more; not talking, not looking, but wrapped in each other as one. In her arms he was not frail. It was their marriage condensed into a single evening. They had no need to speak words. They knew each other's thoughts.

Seeing him now – she was quiet, adoring, and thankful – ended her weeks of awaiting his passing. She cried, but not bitter angry tears, though those would come in time – the anger and sorrow of not having her best friend to touch anymore. These tears were from the joy of countless moments spent together, including moments apart that anticipated physical reunion. She had accepted that he was dying. She had reconciled her soul to what was coming, in the hope of a dignified departing that had been earned by them both. They had been too happy to beweep their "outcast fate and trouble deaf heaven with their bootless cries." They could not dishonor with wailing a life that had made them complete for decades. Her heart ached, but it was full.

Forty years before, she entered that time when the inevitable death of her mother threw her into the situation of a child, a middle-aged child, facing the loss of the last parent. She had weathered her father's death, an event so sudden that she mourned him for months afterward. A car accident took him from her ten years before her mother fell ill with cancer. She didn't fool herself that her mother would pull through: the medicines of the 1920s were no match for certain death. Lives were not routinely prolonged in such circumstances. Cancer was death. She steeled herself for this and mourned only her mother's agony. The death itself was a relief for both of them. Death was dearer then, when ready cures weren't thought of or available.

Though she had braced for her husband's death, it was less tortured than either of her parents' passings. Her husband was in the ever-quickening race to his conclusion. He was eighty-one years old, a point at which people's hearts stopped working and they went. They both knew it was on a swift horizon, the first dim glimpse of which didn't terrify them. Rather than mourn what was to be, she had prepared to miss him. She refused to curse fate.

Now many things needed to be done and details arranged. That would wait. She wanted him still here with her for a bit more. Inside her, there would never be a silence about him. He would be home forever.

Their tidy co-op apartment off Northern Boulevard, in a giant seventeen building development, was theirs since it was erected in 1951. That made ten years of being secure within the four walls, the ceilings and floors, a castle of easy chairs and rounded tables, a busy kitchen, and an inviting bed.

She wanted their place to continue to be filled with him – his coming back and shedding his coat and shoes; his sly smile and exaggerated wink; his laughter from the living room as she fixed dinner; the scent of his shaving lotion; his imprint in the recliner; his shelves of books. She required these to continue to survive the missing of his physical presence.

Wandering away from him, at rest in their bed, she surveyed room by room. In every place, around walls and in front of windows, in closets and hallways, there he was. His raincoat on the rack next to the front door: he'd worn it three days ago when they walked to the small park between the co-op buildings. She sniffed the collar and there he was, sweaty, manly, and alluring. She touched the spines of his books and took one off the shelf. Opening its pages, she found his fingerprint in a grease stain on one. She was reassured that he existed, not forgotten.

He needed to be left alone for the time being, while she needed to sit in his chair and think of him. Next to her was the radio that provided them with the soothing background for their home life, playing the music of their romance. She turned it on and it blanketed her with the sounds of that song again.

They want us to leave. Not just yet. We'll be together in a dream, holding each other.

A tiny speck of the world would remember him, her Kenneth Stuart Doll; a tiny speck knew him. Their children did or thought they did. They knew his love and decency. That was a big part of who he was, but not all of him. He made his fair share of earnest mistakes, though never thoughtless ones. They rarely saw his anger, a distant volcano with a long fuse that erupted in extraordinary conditions. It did erupt, but when it did, it wasn't loud: it was deep, sharp, and incisive. It did erupt, though not at this family but at the outside world. Ken didn't tolerate injustice, and not just particularly general injustice: race against race, rich and poor. Ken hated individual, personal injustice; the injustice of a weaker person being put upon by a stronger entity. He fought for individuals who had to have an ally equal to the size of their opponent. Those were his crusades, carried out with his organized method and single purpose. A neighbor being pushed around by some dismissive bureaucrat soon found Ken's attention to the fight. Ken didn't always win, not that winning in these situations could be defined clearly. Ken gave as he got and exited the battle only after some measure of equity was achieved. Once at someone's side, Ken stayed through to the conclusion. People who hadn't known him came to admire him, both allies and foes, for his resolve.

He loved living, and being his partner, she learned better how to love it too. They were champions together, tasting life for its worth and constantly expanding their experiences. To her, Ken was Don Quixote, perhaps tilting at windmills now and then, and she was his willing

Dulcinea. The sheen of his armor cast stars in her eyes.

If mourning was going to eventually try to overtake her, her thanksgiving for sharing every minute with him was going to beat mourning, without question.

When she spoke at his memorial service, she said in her modest way that they were both in their eighties and life had taken Ken too soon. "There was so much ahead of us. Our best years yet to be lived. Every year was the best year. I have no regrets about either how we lived or Ken's death. We are given a time to take our journey. The journey will take a turn. We go toward a destination from which we will not come back. That part of our journey is unique for each of us, just like our lives up to that point. In his last two days on earth, Ken didn't speak, not to me, not at all. Words never really defined our love. He was getting his bearings on a new road. I loved him before. I loved him then, and I continue to love him. So should you all. Thank you for being with us through the journey."

After the graveside, she went home by herself. She waved off offers of company. She sat in his chair and inhaled him again. She turned on the radio and heard Ella, in her smiling voice, sing about the little happy spots and quirks that were love. How they added up over life.

The telephone rang. Though she hesitated to answer, she did so with her instinct about who might be reaching out to her. Indeed, it was Ken's younger brother. He told her he knew she wasn't at a place for a deep conversation, but he wanted her to know that he was ready when she was to give her his ear and, if wanted, his shoulder. He had always been as peaceful and considerate as his brother Ken. She thanked him for his thoughtfulness and sincerity and said goodbye.

When she glanced at the bookshelves, a yellow box wedged between the tops of some books and the shelf above caught her eye. She thought and recognized what it was. She stood, approached it, and pulled it out. An unwrapped box of imported chocolates, exquisite dark chocolates, of the kind Ken liked – not too sweet, but not too bitter. She opened the box and studied its contents. It was one-third full. Ken had been at it in the weeks before his final decline.

She removed one deep coffee-brown morsel and sat back down. She was going to eat it, not in one chew and swallow, but nip by nip, as she hummed with Ella's voice. Dear Ella. Her eyes welled. She felt Ken's body heat in his chair. She would have another one tomorrow. At the proper time, she might share them with someone else. Right now, they were for her, alone.

The bitter and the sweet lay gently, overlapping on her tongue.

CHAPTER ELEVEN

Who Will Help Them?

Graniteville, Staten Island, September 3, 2003

Here I stand. I can do no other.
Martin Luther

Paul came and sat for a talk. Though it was friendly, some of what he said hit me in the pit of my stomach, but he spoke from love, with deep conviction and an unstoppable faith, as if he were sitting in front of me the entire time.

He was so filled with youth that his beautiful eyes were clear blue beacons, welcoming me into his heart. I so admired him and was thankful for his gracious visit with me at this moment – he was forty-nine and would never see fifty. His spirit was so alive, I was captured by him and his thoughts and pulled deeply into his heroic soul. What manner of person was he? In a world of shallow pools, he was an ocean.

"Paul, why?"

"Would you want to be protected if you were going to be killed, to have your skull punctured or your neck snapped? Would you call me friend or brother if I could stop that and I didn't? If I love you, I will protect you, as you would protect yourself if you could. Isn't that love, to lay down your life for another?"

"The world is against you."

"The world isn't where my heart is. The world is cheap and mean, it loves itself and what it can own. I don't love the world – I love the people in the world, not of the world. I love the children in the world. I love the innocent, the frail, the meek, the defenseless. I stand my life for them. You're a mother, you have children . . ."

"Yes . . ."

"And you love and care for them, against the world, the best you can?"

"Without hesitation. They are my life."

"They are, and your reward is their safety and love and God's love, being a good and faithful servant."

"Yes, that and that they will live on after me. They are . . . a loan. I don't own them. They've been lent to me for a time and then I pass away and they live on, to be and do the same, in turn, for their children."

"I am the same. Shouldn't all the children who are innocent and harmless, shouldn't the most harmless be all our children? A child cannot defend himself. We must."

We regarded each other. I wasn't capable of what he was capable. I was able but not capable. I couldn't do what he had done. I couldn't. He was stronger than I was.

We sat silently for a time. Outside my windows and walls was my neighborhood. It was a quiet one. I stared out my window. My neighbors didn't break rules; they kept clean streets and neat homes and confided in themselves. If you needed help, they were there for you, no one had to prompt them. We lived in harmony. If someone got a bit noisy or tipsy in public, we helped her or him home and no one spoke of it afterward. We looked out for one another. We knew that was what we were supposed to do because our parents had done that, and their parents before them.

Sixty-one years ago, a huge explosion devastated my neighborhood. Buildings on fire and leveled, five people blown apart. A fireworks factory on Richmond Avenue exploded and rained hell on the unsuspecting. Nobody talks about that incident now; hardly anyone knows it happened. We wanted to forget and we did, so it's as if it never happened. But it did, and it can't be wished away by silence. Silence doesn't heal. It doesn't protect. It can't cure an ill or change the truth. Our silence doesn't stop the suffering of the innocent. Polite company isn't an excuse for turning away from the terrors of the world. It's there in front of us even when we close our eyes. Paul wouldn't close his eyes. He wouldn't let me either.

"When I took that first step," Paul related, "I walked over the threshold and on the other side was all that I needed and all I have now, like the man who said 'finish the race.'

"Michael. John. James. Scott. Robert. George. Donald." Paul recited their names. "They can't be of this world, just in it with eyes open." I knew them. They also took the step. A spiritually lost part of society is desensitized to human life. They go blind at the killing of innocent life but cry over the death of a pet. Paul took his step, set down his swift sword, and waited calmly for the world to take him, his faith intact. "To neglect the right of these people to be defended is a sin of immense proportions, with many dire circumstances. Simon Peter cut off Malchus's ear when

Christ was arrested. Do you believe that Peter's act of violence will be judged on equal terms with a doctor puncturing a baby's skull because both acts are wrong?"

Paul had an appointment made for him by others, and he wouldn't miss it. In an awful way, he looked forward to it in comforting anticipation. He wore his Nessus shirt proudly as he went to his judgment.

"I'm going now. I'll see you again soon. In no time, really. We'll sit and talk again. Goodbye, dear friend. Not so many people would give me their time like this. You know. Your heart is ready. It's open. The world may judge you. It will hate you because you have time for me. That's fine. You are better to be seen with your friends than shunned by everyone else. The friends, like you and me, will endure beyond the world. The others will go somewhere apart. I'll greet you, sister, in my new home soon."

He bent his head, those blue eyes lowered for a second, then looked up and smiled, a smile he gave his own three children, ages three, six, and nine. I wasn't able to lose him like this, though he was already gone and never here. His children lost him, though they never let go and neither did he. I looked out my window and he was gone. I didn't let go. I see him to this day, with those clear blue eyes and the flame behind them.

Paul believed. He knew there was no sin too big for forgiveness and grace. If the devil itself sincerely repented and asked, it could attain salvation. But, compromising with evil, permitting it in silence is a sin.

There is a difference between doing evil for evil's purposes and preventing evil. They are neither equal nor morally equivalent. Hate and love are not the same because they're both powerful emotions. The strength to more than resist evil but to eliminate it, to defend others and subdue their tormentors, that strength is rare. At times, we are pushed into using that strength, that will, against our will and our better natures when we are called to war. There are a few whose conscience propels them to take the first step and stand against what will be, not solely what has been or is. They are called zealots and fanatics because they don't wait for someone else to be harmed, they prevent it from happening or continuing to happen. They change the world against its will, with a higher will and a righteous purpose. They are fire, setting the world ablaze with a consecrated spark.

A lofty army exists, one that is action, not all talk; a subterranean passage for the innocent against their terrorizers. That army is on a wholehearted mission, not one of hands alone, but also spirit, soul, and wisdom. I couldn't understand John Brown until I knew that he aimed to create a place where there were no more people willing and able to bury the terrorists, because he was not one of them – he was their implacable enemy, seized by his mission. Knowing this truth, I took Paul's hands and shook the dust off them, because others would not receive him. On his way to his appointment, Paul remarked to no one in particular, "This is a beautiful country." John Brown had made the same remark.

Paul went on. He said, "Protect them as you would be protected. Truth and righteousness will prevail." I saw Paul in the images of fallen soldiers who gave their lives battling evil. Paul went on to make the innocent free. Wrath must have an instrument to wield its lightning and shield. Paul was a willing instrument, a joyous one. The killers were praised in death as innocent, as innocent as their victims, who were forgotten in silence since no one wants to remember the unspeakable acts or call them by their right name. The killing of the most innocent is not a right: it is murder. Innocent human life doesn't belong in chains or a surgical garbage pail. Paul was vilified by the world. His name is still spoken in a hush. Like John Brown's, it is still spoken.

CHAPTER TWELVE

The Shark Bites

Maspeth, Queens, January 10, 1984

*Compassion is the keen awareness of the
interdependence of all things.*
Thomas Merton

Bartending is a profession, one that I practiced, successfully I might add, for over twenty-five years. A professional bartender, not a fly-by-night part-time huckster or college kid in for a buck, knows his business, his booze, and his customers. Or hers, as the case may be. I've known as many female professional bartenders as male.

If you're honest with your owner and the people at the bar, you're a rare and valuable worker. If I went out now, ten years after my last bar gig, and sought work, one hundred out of one hundred places where I applied would hire me on the spot. I am that good.

You see, ordinary bartenders, left to their own devices, will rob a bar owner blind. They can't help it; it is their nature. Dozens and dozens of thirsty customers, half of them drunk and many of them on the make, all of them wanting service immediately. Mixed drinks and beers flying across the bar and cash flying in the other direction, who can keep track? The bartenders do. They know each order and they don't let anyone get away without paying, except the periodic buyback for a repeat good customer. That is allowed, even encouraged as good for business by the owner.

But bartenders in a hectic situation will start giving the house ten for the register and one in the pocket, in addition to tips. With fast bartenders serving hundreds of drinks per night, that becomes a healthy little side income. Unless someone is watching them in action, you'll never find out until they've moved on to their next gig, like all bartenders eventually do. That was my number one job as head bartender, to stop the theft before it got rolling.

During the daytime in a neighborhood bar like my last place, older customers would come in, sit, and have a beer and a shot. The nearest I came to serving a mixed drink in the daytime was a glass of seasoned tomato juice (always Sacramento because it was so thick) with a shot of vodka. One old man, he looked sober but was actually a bad rummy, drank a Bloody Mary with a Fleischmann's whiskey chaser, ten or twelve in a row nonstop. He said the tomato juice was his lunch! He never stumbled. He could hold his liquor.

In the evening, the bar became a social place where neighbors mixed with newcomers and single men sought single women, who looked to be sought. Every night except Sunday when we were closed, the bar was a scene with plenty of scores.

Lots of other stuff went on in the bar in addition to drinking and flirting. The owner was seldom there, meaning I ran the whole business most of the time.

Thousands of dollars passed into and out of my hands, and I was paid a healthy salary, plus tips. I was worth it and then some, taking into account the hundreds of dollars of bar receipts that wouldn't be stolen on a nightly basis. The owner knew what he had in me, and I liked what I did for a living. Business marriage made in heaven. A number of other people plied their trade in the bar too; vendors, you could call them.

There was Jimmy John, the bookie. Bookies are a lot like insurance companies. They make their money off you coming and going, and they lay off their excess action to avoid big payoffs. Jimmy John was part of a crew and he paid a tax to the bar owner for the privilege of taking action in my place. Jimmy John was a regular guy, laid back, never got worked up about anything. After all, when a bettor won, Jimmy John took a piece, and when one lost, Jimmy John got his money plus the fee for betting with him. He had flaming red hair and freckles. Jimmy John was the product of a mom from County Cork and a Calabrese dad.

Another vendor was Frankie Suits. He sold suits out of the back of his royal blue Lincoln Mark III, with the white leather interior and the Cartier clock on the dash. Of course, the suits, which ranged from imported polyester to Bloomingdale's best, were either hijacked or stolen off the docks. Once a week, Frankie would come into the bar about noon time and announce he had a new shipment. His prices were fair and not all my daytime drinkers were rummies, so he did quite a low overhead/high profit, traveling business.

Then there was Billy Cee, an Irishman. He was a loan shark. Squat, about five feet, six inches, with a massive square torso and receding jet-black hair. He wore thick glasses. His lower body didn't match his overdeveloped upper, so he walked with a slight hitch, also because he was once shot in the butt while fleeing a robbery he was committing. Billy loaned money to the small businessmen who couldn't get a bank loan, the hopeless gamblers, the poor souls who were so far in debt they could barely lift their heads above water, and other unfortunates. They came to the bar on weekday mornings to pay their installments. What a pathetic bunch. Billy would have them meet him at the bar and then take them into the men's room to hand over the cash. Billy felt comfortable transacting in the toilet. I guess he believed no one would wiretap a bathroom. The bar owner looked the other way for a nice monthly fee.

Loan-sharking is tough business. The shark is responsible for the money he lends out on the street, but that money usually comes from someone above him, someone who has to answer to someone else, and everybody demanding accounting to the penny. Shark money has to move, keep circulating, collecting interest at huge rates, being paid back, with no deadbeats. That is a fit description because if you try to run out on a shark and his money, you're dead. I advise you, never get in bed with a shark. You can't win. It is better to stiff a bank or your uncle than not pay a shark.

Billy Cee prospered in his line of work. Me, I put some of my money with Billy and let him handle it. A very sound investment. A way to grow the green. My Irish-Castilian father, who had no money to speak of, would say, "Money is round and meant to roll!" I think he learned that from one of our Italian neighbors.

Billy was no soft touch. His customers paid up, occasionally with a little forceful encouragement. He didn't forgive his debtors. But from my point of view, there were folks I didn't care to see give him any action.

I'll tell you how much I'm against certain people going to a loan shark. I'm behind the bar one afternoon and a man comes in, looking very hesitant. Billy catches his eye and looks him on to a stool. Billy's about to go into the bathroom with a loser, who I recognize from many previous trips to the john with Billy. This repeat loser might as well rent the toilet bowl from the owner because he's going to be there until he dies. The man who walked in is now parked in the waiting room, my bar, for his turn.

He sits at the bar and asks me if he can have a glass of water. Most of my customers don't ask, they order, and it isn't just water. I'm looking at him. Neatly dressed and shaved, with a clean haircut and a properly knotted tie. I saw his shoes when he walked in – shined. This is not a person who should be doing anything with a shark. He's nervous too. Like his asking for water. He's out of place here. I start wondering what's his story.

I'm trying not to stare but I keep looking back at him while I pour beers for the bar residents. Why is a person like this about to begin that protracted, slow slide into the quicksand that will take his wallet, his soul, and ultimately wreck him? It doesn't figure.

Then, it hits me. I know him. Not now but when he and I were teenagers. In the ninth grade, he was two years ahead of me. I didn't know him from public school but RI, religious instruction. We were "publics": our parents didn't enroll us in Catholic school, either because they couldn't afford it, as in my case, or they didn't believe it was necessary, which was probably his reason. "Publics" got let out early from public school to attend religious classes on school time. He was in my RI class.

Vinny? No, Benny. No, Timmy. Yeah, Timmy. Timothy Gallagher. The priest always read out our full names. Timothy Gallagher. His dad was a clerk in the bank, the bank where my parents deposited my communion money and the gifts from my aunts and uncles. My parents' bank. I remember it because it was a bus trip to get there and the inside of the bank was this giant dome. An impressive place. It had giant dimes carved in the ceiling. My parents told me they put their money there because the bank president was a Catholic. I met Timmy there once when he was visiting his father, who sat at one of the desks. I guess his old man wasn't a teller; he must have been a bank officer.

What was Timmy Gallagher doing at my bar, meeting with Billy Cee?

"Hey Timmy, remember me? From Epiphany?"

He gave me this strange look. He was embarrassed. Embarrassed to be in bar on a weekday during working hours, recognized by someone from his past.

Probably embarrassed to be waiting for a loan shark.

"Yeah, hi. Yeah, I didn't recognize you."

Yes, you do.

"Timmy, how ya been?" *Not so good, I'm guessing.*

"Yeah, okay. Okay, I guess."

You guess because you're in something and now you know that I know you got it on you and it stinks. Something doesn't add up. Regular fellow with a squeaky-clean father, and a wedding band with likely a goody two shoes wife. Visiting a loan shark in a bar.

I drew up close to him over the bar. It didn't matter – the rest of my customers at that hour were drunks passed out on their stools.

"Timmy. Don't take it wrong but whataya doing here?"

He couldn't look me in the eye. He knew what I was seeing in him, and he didn't want me to know.

"I'm . . . I'm seeing Billy."

"Timmy, you know I manage this place?"

"Yeah." So, he did recognize me.

"I know what Billy does for a living. Whataya doing here?"

He did not want to answer. For him, at this point, it was like taking off all his clothes in public.

But he did. "I need some help."

"You need some money, right?"

"I need help. I'm in a jam."

"Is that jam gambling, booze, or a woman?"

He looked me in the eye for the first time.

"No. None of those. My wife got in trouble at her job. I have to help her."

"How much trouble?" I wasn't going to beat around the bush, even his wife's. Trouble he couldn't go to his father's banker pals for help?

He couldn't say it out loud. He was straining. For some reason – old friendship, the Church, my not wanting to watch a young man drown – I handed him my pen and a napkin. He looked at me, then at the pen and paper, then back at me. I was no saint, not then, not now. This wasn't about my being nice to him, really. It was not wanting this to happen in my place when I could do something about it.

Once in a while, you're supposed to help your fellow

man and remember what your mother told you. Maybe not always, but once in a while.

He looked down and slowly wrote on the napkin. He looked up at me.

On the napkin he wrote "1,000."

One thousand dollars. He was going to get himself bled dry for a lousy grand. That number was meaningless to me but to him, it was his life. Mr. Straight Arrow.

One thousand dollars. A stinking, measly grand. If I wanted to, I could wipe my ass with a thousand dollars and barely miss it.

He must have truly loved his wife. I wasn't going to think about what she did that cost a thousand dollars borrowed from a loan shark, that in the end would cost more than five times that amount. I knew enough to never put a finger between a married couple.

I dug into my pocket. My everyday walking around money was a lot more than a grand. I peeled off the bills, ten hundreds, and gave it to him, on the bar. He looked at me, asking *why* without speaking.

"Religious instruction. 'Thou shalt not steal.' Don't mess with loan sharks," I answered his look out loud.

Maybe he didn't know what to say. This wasn't what he thought would occur. I wanted him to leave. I'd deal with Billy.

He wanted to say thanks, but the words weren't there. I broke the awkward silence.

"Timmy. When you can, pay me back. No interest. I'm not a shark. I'm a bartender."

"I can't know when . . . I don't . . ."

"Go. Go back to your wife. I'll see ya when I see ya."

He stood up, looked at the bar, I mean looked right

down at the bar as if a miracle happened, and then walked out the door, with the hundreds still in his hand. I hoped he put them in his pocket; no knowing who might walk by and try to take it, out in the open like that.

Billy came back to the bar, looking for his next customer.

"Hey, Billy," I called, "he left. Must have lost his nerve."

"His loss. He'll be back."

Sharks. Always looking for somebody bleeding.

Me – I knew no good deed goes unpunished. This would rebound on me. His not-so-clean wife might nag him about borrowing from a bartender, like my profession was dirty or beneath her, them. Who cared what she might think? I hadn't stolen my money. It was earned on the up and up. What was she hiding and her husband covering up for her? I had no expectation of gratitude from either of them.

My dad told me to never judge what a man and a woman had together. The ones that were all over each other in public usually went home and tried to kill each other. It was an act. The ones that snarled at each other in public were hot lovers behind closed doors. Anger and passion were more than kissing cousins.

The point is, no one knows why we act the way we do except ourselves, and then, if we're being honest, there are things we do that we can't explain.

It may sound odd, coming from a past middle-aged man, but I found that I lived my life with my mother's words in my ears. "Help the little guy when you can because you're the little guy sometimes. Don't do it because you want a thank-you. Do it because it's right."

I must have been nine, and mom read this to me:

Sympathy sees and says, "I'm sorry." Compassion sees and says, "I'll help." I remember her voice. She was right, always right. Bless her.

CHAPTER THIRTEEN

Civic Duties

Brooklyn Heights, Brooklyn, September 29, 1977

Have the courage to make use of your own reason.
Immanuel Kant

The union was good to me, I have no complaints. For a high school graduate, by the skin of my teeth, I hooked a city job as clerk and put in my eight hours. For ten years I stuck to it, on time every day, never out sick, few vacations, kept my head down, and followed the rules.

Then a man called me aside at work. I knew about him: Tommy Roberti was the union local president, and he was recruiting organizers to grow the local. He liked how I handled myself and more importantly, he liked that I was physically large, no wife, half a brain, and very determined. He'd been watching me, he said. "How would you like to become a steward and help me? This thing is getting bigger, and workers like you will make us stronger."

Sounded all right to me. I definitely didn't want to be a clerk forever, and I welcomed a challenge. I accepted.

The next five years, I did what the union needed to be

done. A member had a beef with a supervisor, I represented the member and made a deal with management. A manager was leaning on a member for being ten minutes late to work a number of times a week: I leaned on the manager to lighten up. Contract negotiations were stalled. I'm one of the brawny negotiators who never said a word but sat at the table to intimidate the bosses.

Then the asks became more personal. The local loaned a few grand to a unionized business in trouble. Under the table. The business stopped making payments. I went and convinced the debtor to open the cash register and get up to date on the loan. A bully tried to force the local president's daughter to date him. I visited the kid and he landed in the hospital the next day. He stayed a month and didn't talk.

Fall 1977, right after Labor Day, Tommy told me we were going to lunch in Brooklyn Heights at Foffe's to meet an old friend.

Foffe's was a one-of-a-kind restaurant. It was started by an Italian widow and her nine sons. It became an institution on Montague Street, serving Italian food and specializing in game caught by Alfred Foffe, one of the widow's sons who was a noted hunter. He ran the place with his brother John. After the hunt, Alfred would hang some of his catch in front to announce wild game was being served. You could walk by and see a buck and several grouse suspended outside of the second-floor windows. It was a meeting place for many famous Brooklynites, on both sides of the law, but a fancy meeting place. It wasn't cheap.

There was a Foffe's branch in Bay Ridge, nowhere near as famous or popular as the original in the Heights.

What friend Tommy would have at Foffe's I did not know. I did know that half the judges in Brooklyn ate there on a regular basis, and most of them got their jobs sitting at Foffe's tables. A lot of political business was done over roast venison steaks.

Entering Foffe's was entering a time about sixty years earlier. The wood-paneled walls, thick carpets, and soft velvet chairs were lit by sconces (yeah, I knew what sconces were). The waiters wore starched white aprons.

A bull-faced man holding a cigar, seated at a table in the window called us over.

"Tommy!"

"Mataeo!" Tommy answered.

He and Tommy hugged. Two Italians showing respect.

"Mataeo, I want to introduce my friend John Emma."

Mataeo put a clutch on my hand, not enough to give me pain but plenty strong. He was older than me by a wide margin, but he was fit and tough.

Mataeo once said he had forty-two judges in his pocket. I heard of him. The Old Roman of Kings County. The Democrat General of Brooklyn. The kingmaker.

"Sit. Sit," he ordered us.

A sharp dresser with a pencil mustache rushed over to the table. I realized he was Alfred, one of the owners.

"Tommaso! How good to see you return. Too long."

Out of thin air, waiters, plural, swarmed around us, holding our chairs, unfurling our napkins onto our laps, pouring water, extending menus.

Alfred spoke up. "No menus for my guests Mataeo and Tommy. And . . .?"

He was looking for my name.

"John. John Emma." Usually, I wouldn't say my name

out loud in public, but Foffe's seemed safe enough for Tommy and his friend Mataeo, so I did.

Alfred responded, "John Emma? So, you are *Sicilianu*?"

"My father's side."

"I can tell. Enna. On the hill. That is where your people are from, right?"

Damned if he wasn't right. There are Italians like this. Their heritage is such a thing of beauty that they've traced the roots of family names and can tell you within a town or two where your family is from. That's Italian pride.

"You're correct. On the hilltop."

"Yes, yes. A magnificent place. Please, I will order for you all."

He actually snapped his fingers to summon a waiter with pad and pencil ready and gave our order in Italian. It was said pretty quickly, but I did make out the word for eel, *anguilla*, and *in umido*, so eels in a tomato and wine sauce: a traditional Neapolitan dish, eaten to conquer the devil, as represented by the snake (eel) that ruined Adam and Eve. I heard "pompano" too. I liked both dishes.

Tommy looked at me while talking to his friend Mataeo.

"John is the one I go to when I need something done right." He was smiling.

Mataeo looked me in my eyes. "John, I've heard nothing but good about you." I wondered from where, but he didn't hesitate to explain. "I've been around Brooklyn forever, I'm like Borough Hall – always there when you need me. I know a lot of people. I know lots of folks in your neighborhood. They say you're a good neighbor, decent, ready to help others. You're honest. Nothing but good about you."

Mataeo asked me, "John, you follow politics?"

"Sorry, no. I'm busy most of the time."

"No problem, I don't expect young people to be up on everything like us old folks. You know we're having an election for mayor in six weeks?"

That I did know because an Italian, Cuomo, was running against a Jewish congressman.

"Yes, that but not much else."

"John" – Mataeo put his massive hand on my forearm gently – "you might think an old Italian like me would be pushing for a fellow countryman. Not this time. We had an Italian mayor before, actually two. Fiorello and Impy. The first one was good, but that second one, Impy, he couldn't think normal; he let his parks commissioner run the city. No, I'm not for the Italian this time, I'm for the Jew. The congressman is a solid fellow. Plays ball. Knows the score. He once ousted a friend of mine, Carmine in the Village, but I forgive him. After eight years of that Lindsay, the Matinee Idol I call him, dumb as dirt, and four years of my friend Abe, it's time for a change. The congressman won the runoff and the governor asked Cuomo to step aside, but he's going to run on the Liberal line. I call it the whore line. They sell themselves to the highest bidder. But once you're bought, it's honorable to stay bought! You'll see, Cuomo's not going to honor those whores. He'll try to take the party over because he is one himself."

He stopped because the eel in sauce was delivered to our table.

"You know," he continued after a forkful of eel, which was delicious, "in the primary, the congressman didn't win any one of the five boroughs, but he polled strong enough in each to come in first overall, eleven thousand votes ahead of Cuomo. That shows me the congressman has wide voter appeal and can stay on maybe one or two terms more. He talks, acts, and looks like a New Yorker. Cuomo's a college boy from Queens. If he holds on, he can be lieutenant governor to our boy Carey, then run for governor himself. The governor asked him to step aside after the primary, but he wouldn't listen. His people are from Campania, you know, ran a grocery in Queens. Did a little business on the side."

Tommy was listening, eating, and smiling throughout the story. He put down his fork and spoke. "Mataeo, sometimes it's your own kind that give you the most trouble!" He winked at me.

Mataeo, still working on his eel, spoke again.

"Isn't that the truth? Remember Red Mike Quill? He quit the commies and said, 'You thought you were using me, when all the while it was me using you!' If you knew the problems I have in Albany. Now the governor, he's as sweet as bread. Irish. Never gives me a moment's trouble. Brooklyn boy. What a nice man and educated. He likes Cuomo anyway, so I'm going to have to forgive Mario, but not before I crush his nuts in this election. He's too smart, needs a lesson. He belongs on the Supreme Court, the top one. Not New York politics."

"Mataeo, why don't I tell John the favors we need?" That "we need" was interesting. Mataeo and Tommy were definitely deep in business together. I wondered what Mataeo did on the side to take advantage of his political power.

Tommy spoke softly. "Mataeo and his friends are from the Monroe Club in Brooklyn. That's how he knows about you. During the election, they have some projects that you can absolutely help them with. For one, there's the Brooklyn Senior Italian Committee. They help our old folks vote. See, the seniors, for them getting up, dressing for the weather, going to the polls, and standing in line is not fair. They paid their dues and they want to be good Americans. The committee fills out their ballots for them, gets their signatures, and delivers the votes to the polls."

Mataeo interjected while the fish was being served, "We're talking thousands of votes here."

"Yeah, big job. John, you can help by organizing the work, guarding the ballots on the way, and ensuring there are no slipups. Now, there's also the absentee ballots. These folks can't get to the voting place on Election Day for one reason or another, so you work with the Monroe Club to see everyone gets an absentee ballot, fills it in the right way, and it gets delivered, hand delivered to the Elections Board."

Mataeo cut in again. "Then there's the votes from those who passed."

Tommy picked up, "Right. See, some poor folks die right before the election but they're good citizens, they want to vote too . . ."

"Been voting for decades now. Why deprive them of their last chance to be a loyal citizen?" Mataeo added.

Tommy continued, "Right. We do honor to the deceased and help our city. It's good civics like they taught us in school. See, John, you're helping in the democracy."

If the two of them hadn't been so dead serious, I would have exploded laughing. Clearly, they were in cahoots doing these things for years. I was this Election Day's elf, probably because I solved the bully problem so neatly. Mataeo set it all on the table. "I want to teach Cuomo a good lesson. I want Brooklyn to crush him at the polls. When your governor tells you to step aside, do it!"

Well, I was all for civic duty and democracy and shoving it down Cuomo's throat, if that's what Tommy, and my new friend Mataeo, wanted.

"My pleasure to help, Mataeo." I stuck out my hand, and he took it in his big paw like I was handing him a couple of grand in large bills.

"John, I'm pleased I met you." He turned his face to Tommy. "There's something real nice in this for John, right, Tommy?"

"Oh, of course. I take care of John. He's practically my right hand."

"By the way," Mataeo put in, "I understand that you're quite a hunter yourself, like Alfred."

I smiled. He was joking and meant the bully I gave a beating. "I've bagged a couple of six-pointers," I responded.

We completed our pleasant lunch with biscotti and glasses of Amaro Averna.

Up to Election Day and then some, I proved my worth as a friend to Mataeo and the Monroe Club. I made sure every vote was counted, some twice. The dead voted faithfully Democrat. Along the way, I met interesting people, political people you might say who weren't well known but were very effective in what they did.

Take Pete the Mechanic, for example. Pete was in the perfect job for his special talent. He was an employee of the New York City Board of Elections. Everybody at the board got a job through either the Democrat bosses in the city, the few Republican bosses, or an agreement between them. Pete was bought, owned, and paid for by Mataeo. In his job as Elections Board mechanic, Pete fixed the voting machines. He fixed them good. In certain districts in Brooklyn, he fixed them so that every third Republican or Liberal Party vote for mayor registered for the Democrat candidate. In other districts, with significant Republican or Liberal Party registration, he fixed the machines so that they stopped registering votes correctly after a certain number was reached. All votes after that number became Democrat votes. Pete was one of Mataeo's favorites.

I learned what WAM was. WAM was "walking around money," the bankrolls certain political workers carried with them in election season and especially on voting day to meet the immediate needs of voters eager to pull the lever for the right candidate. WAM would be delivered in batches of cash to places in the community, like churches and senior centers, then parceled out to local leaders. If a voter, for example, needed five bucks to cover babysitting because the hubby was out on a drunk Election Day, the WAM covered the situation. WAM might buy a bag of groceries or a tank of gas. The aim was to get that voter to the polls. This was considered a noble public service. Mataeo told me a very rich multiterm Republican governor of New York was famous in political circles for the amount of WAM he provided every four years, with Mount Carmel Church in East Harlem one of the governor's favorite drop spots. The parish took its tithe.

Maybe some of this sounds like cheating to you? It was, but it was available to both sides. The Cuomo bunch used a particularly nasty little gimmick on the congressman – a rhyme that went, "Vote for Cuomo, not the homo." Even nastier is Cuomo denied he did it. So, he was a liar on top of it all. For me, that is a far piece worse than handing out money. I came to see Cuomo as a first-class ass. I was overjoyed to help him lose. It was a pleasure. Cuomo was what Mataeo said he was, a whore. A vindictive whore. His son was part of that campaign. I imagined what this son of a whore would be like in a few years. Several years later like Mataeo predicted, senior Cuomo tried to take over the Liberal Party. He failed, but eventually drove it out of New York elections. A vindictive whore.

The congressman from Manhattan became mayor of New York City with over thirty-one thousand more votes in Brooklyn than Cuomo. Interestingly enough, after the election, my relations with the cops in Brooklyn improved, though they were pretty good before then. The word got around that Mataeo and I were friends.

I learned Mataeo was in the insurance brokerage business and all the insurance needs for Tommy's union local were handled by him.

I dined at Foffe's occasionally after that lunch, and I never was presented with a check. Though I never performed Election Day duties again, I started following local politics. I suspect Mataeo recruited one elf per election so that no one caught on to all his secrets. That disappointed me to a degree because my one taste inside the game was an eye-opener. Regular people didn't see what I saw and did. It was different, though I think I might have been sucked in too far if I had continued. I was better off looking from the outside in instead of the other way around. If I had seen it all up close over time, I would have concluded all politicians were superficial pricks and worthless sacks of shit. Now, I thought they were a nest of vipers. Get too close and you're poisoned.

I suppose every election is a crooked deal and the

winner is the bigger crook. Other crooks went to jail and politicians got on TV, and that was accepted and proper. Every four years there was a heist and we looked the other way: nothing to see here, keep moving.

My life was steady, normal, given I did some iffy things in the union line of work. Like I said, I finished high school one step ahead of my teachers and the guidance counselor. Election rigging, if you want to call it that, was an experience I wouldn't forget, but it wasn't me. In my union steward position, I helped the little guy against the bosses. Who did I help by stuffing ballot boxes? Certainly not the little guy.

I made a nice sum for my Election Day troubles, meaning the troubles I helped cause others. Thinking about it afterward, that was like blood money, the reward for taking something by trickery to give to someone else who didn't work for it, with a crumb or two left over for me. It was dirty money. Not my way of earning my daily bread. Another union steward once warned me, "Lie down with dogs, wake up with fleas." That struck me. The politicians were flea-bitten, mangy mutts, and I wasn't going to be.

CHAPTER FOURTEEN

Miles Live!

Upper West Side, Manhattan, October 7, 1986

Do what is more difficult & more brave.
Julia Sand, writing to Chester A. Arthur

Miles Davis spoke in a whisper. Years before, he had argued forcefully with his doctors about his treatment after an operation and succeeded in permanently damaging his vocal cords.

Here he was in front of a packed studio audience, dressed in a dark sequined jacket, loads of gold jewelry, dazzling striped harem pants, and, naturally, dark glasses, carrying his red horn and seated with the host on stage, after playing a driving jazz number with the band. The sound was round, moving in a beat of half notes, the vibrato cutting the notes at a fierce speed. But it was so mellow that the hushed audience shook with the rhythm. This was the Miles democracy: each musician had his turn, all of them contributing to the sway, and Miles sometimes off to the side to blow, his horn tilted low, sometimes on the keyboard and other times strolling forward and back, always in time with the incredible sound. He was the elegant, sleek metronome.

How I scored admission to the taping of this program, I don't remember. I can't tell you what the name of the song was – it didn't matter. It was Miles, making music, talking softly, being Miles.

Miles was a man whose physicality meant little in terms of his presence, though his smooth skin shone like polished ebony stone. Next to him on the stage sat the host, a famous, pale, and diminutive man, noted for his erudition. In all things that evening, he deferred to Miles, calling him "Mr. Davis." Miles was dominating, and like facing Al Davis's Raiders saying "Pride, Poise, Excellence," being there engendered chills. Miles's energy filled the space he occupied, and the penumbra and the stratosphere. Miles was the music, far above coffee table trivia and chitchat. Miles was.

With obvious reverence, the grinning host intoned, "It's a real treat to have you here."

And Miles was loving it, not hogging it but genuinely loving it. He knew who he was and what he was. A supernova, a hurricane, a thunderbolt, a cry in the wilderness. He was indeed the Prince of Darkness. He was royalty. He was cool and distant, and deep and kind.

One of the other guests, in addition to a coy actress, was a male movie star with considerable box office moxie. Like a schoolboy doofus, he presumed to bring a trumpet on stage with him, in the presence of the master, because he said it "matched" his suit! Miles eyed and sized him up. When this lightweight asked Miles how to hold a horn properly, the Prince demonstrated the grip inherited from his childhood in East St. Louis and chastised the boy for disrespecting the instrument by placing it on the floor immodestly. Then Miles politely told him to sit down and speak when spoken to. The puppy stayed silent thereafter. A king admonishing a fool.

The host questioned Miles on many topics, and Miles responded after contemplation. Did the awe of musicians for him make Miles uncomfortable? Miles replied he had heard drummers dropped their sticks when he entered a room but there was no reason to be nervous "if you know what you're doing." How did Miles move from one musical genre to the next so effortlessly? "I don't try to change music, it happens." And, like a Heisenberg experiment, Miles's involvement turned the music into another, previously unseen reality. Of bassist Percy Heath, whom Miles had encouraged and employed, Miles said, "Good bass player. The Modern Jazz Quartet messed him up." Miles was cutting no corners that evening.

With the host's prompting, Miles recounted the several times he had been stopped by the cops while driving and interrogated about his ownership of his car and the source of his funds to buy it. Miles wagged his beautiful ebony head, his flowing curls going to and fro in frustration at recalling that slice of life. With warmth and kindly humor, the host gave Miles a license plate that read "I OWN IT BABY." Miles was clearly touched by the gift and reached out and held the host's hand. He understood, at least this piece of his existence, the host understood. You have to laugh at times to not cry, but you never forget.

Eighteen years earlier, I was a thirteen-year-old leaning against a pillar in Manhattan's Columbus Circle subway station, waiting for my train back to Brooklyn. Another train, not mine, stopped at the platform and opened its doors. My brain was somewhere else, though I saw the open train door in front of me. I barely made out a tall figure, a man standing in the doorway, facing me. With the door closing, the man spat in my face. The unexpected wetness on my cheek, more than the man's act of spitting, shocked me first. I saw him through the window of the train door, laughing while his train pulled out. I was more confused than angry or hurt. The why of it was such a mystery, to this day, that I didn't speak of it with anyone, not my own parents or friends. Curiously, I was ashamed and embarrassed, though I still can't say for sure why. I hadn't done anything but stand. It was the unknown why that hurt me the most.

Life could be like that – not always, but at times. Being black was often an offense, if not a crime. I suspect that, like Miles, what was done to me wasn't something I would ever do to others or consider doing, though I've ignorantly hurt others, innocent others, by a word I used or a gesture. But not by something I did deliberately to cause pain. The act of spitting on me spoke of the doer, not of me.

I would never see that tormentor again and, if I did, I wouldn't recognize him. I couldn't get back at him or extract primitive justice. I had to live without him in my life, forever after. Life was viciously frustrating if I allowed it to linger on the hurt. Or I could live above and beyond frustration, outside of hate, to the right of stupidity, apart from jealousy and self-pity. Yes, feeling the pain, not being consumed by it. I am not a victim. Victims are losers to the will of their tormentors. "If you know what you're doing," attitude can reshape the disfigured and unknit life's twists and missteps. The pain is a marker.

Pain is the memory of injury, but pain also ushers in

truth. Pain in life is a lamp that lights the honest road ahead, away from victimhood. Going through the pain brings us out better and whole to where no one steals our dignity, that dignity that is rooted in faith. The spitter's judgment of me was meaningless: I had no faith in a person's earthly verdict. He didn't know me or my heart. To believe and live otherwise would give credence and power to the tormentor.

An elderly Jewish man, who in his adolescence witnessed and experienced life's horrors, once told me, "There is dignity in living, not in crying. Living is the answer to cruelty. Put your heart beyond evil and your dignity will overcome it. Do not allow evil to take root in you. Never let anyone sow that seed in your soul."

Miles proclaimed, "Jazz is an attitude." So is dignity. Miles had it, pressed down, shaken up, and overflowing. He was the full measure of dignity.

Miles Dewey Davis III was born in 1926 in Alton, Illinois, and was raised in East St. Louis, Illinois. His father was a prosperous dentist, with his practice located in a white neighborhood; his mother was a music teacher and violinist. Prophetically, Miles attended an elementary school named after a free black man, Crispus Attucks, who was first to be killed in the American Revolution. Miles would lead a different set of revolutions.

Miles was handed a horn in grade school and eventually attended Juilliard in New York, though he dropped out before graduating to enable him to play music with Charlie Parker. He fought protracted battles with heroin and cocaine, sapping his strength and tearing down his health, to eventually defeat them before they killed him. He lived after the battles, scarred but determined.

Through it all, Miles heard what others couldn't hear and advanced relentlessly to the next new day. He developed, wrote, played, improvised, and revolutionized jazz, bebop, funk, pop, ballads, lush orchestrations, modern, postmodern, and post– all else.

That evening in 1986 ended with Miles riffing on another musical number, in a duet with the guitarist, and leaving the audience in that dizzied state of exhaustion and marvelous climax. All Miles, all the way. A piece of the best of him he was sharing was what I hoped for in me.

I was there for his witness in words. I was raised Baptist and recognized the blessing of being in that studio with Miles. It was a sacred honor. It was my witness too. Witness has power; it opens the giver and the receiver to healing. Through Miles's witness, I was opened to at last acknowledge my unspoken wound. I praised Miles for showing his scar, for being hurt as I had been hurt, and coming out on this end, home again and fearless. He wasn't forgetting; to the contrary, he acknowledged an important victory. He shared his spiritual property: life after pain. The tormentors failed.

Am I the sum of my pain or my triumphs over pain? Do I suffer to suffer or for the wisdom and discernment to overcome and be stronger? How strong was my faith?

My faith teaches that witness is the essence of survival through agape, unselfish love, the love that gives life freely for others. Giving witness is ultimate sharing, conscious tithing, the giving of a tenth every moment and doing it with love. This is boundless generosity, giving material possessions and spirit, and no expectation of reward except casting love into the present and beyond.

Ten months earlier, the same host had interviewed

Richard Pryor. Pryor related meeting Louis Armstrong before a joint performance. When asked how he was doing, Armstrong remarked with a sly smile, "White man still in the lead." Louis was tithing what no one could take from him and what he alone could give. Then Richard had it, then me.

CHAPTER FIFTEEN

Let It Be

Rochdale Village, Queens, July 4, 1990

To live will be an awfully big adventure.
J. M. Barrie

The tea isn't hot. How many times have I told Miss Tuttle, the tea must be boiling hot, with a tea cloth over the poured cup and a cozy on the pot? How is one to enjoy one's tea if it's not hot enough? Darjeeling and Assam from Twinings, well and good, but it must be hot!

Where is she? Where is our bell? Miss Tuttle! Miss Tuttle!

Oh my, she must be listening to the radio in the pantry. Naughty girl. Such a bad girl. Well . . . help is what one expects it to be. We mustn't upset ourselves. She'll be here soon, always returning to ask after us and our comforts. She's a good girl, just lazy and forgetful. We'd never sack her, perhaps lightly scold her periodic indolence.

The milk (no cream, no sugar), the bone china with our initials, all perfectly correct. What a pity about the temperature. There we have it – one must make do.

The Dundee cake is scrumptious. Our favorite – tea time is not tea time without our Dundee cake. Keiller's marmalade with currants, sultanas, and almonds, no glacè cherries, never. A treat for one to slice one's own each day.

Such a lovely tray before us – the finger sandwiches without crusts, cut lengthways (like fingers!); smoked salmon from Scotland with dill, egg mayonnaise, and a touch of mustard, and the cucumber ones spread with sweet creamery butter (from our son's dairy). This is our favorite meal of the day for good reason. It is.

We give thanks to Thee for our bounties and Your abiding blessings over our homes and people.

And scones for the corgis, must save them for our little ones.

Where is Miss Tuttle? It's well after five and she's laid this out for us, but where is she?

Mustn't complain. Others suffer so terribly these days; we are blessed. There outside our windows are the salt of this favored earth. Their loyalty and affection keep one going. How we care for them. They walk about the gardens and around Constitution Hill, so industrious and behaved. Civil. That's the proper term, civil. They're civil. These lands depend on them. We serve them and they honor us with their service and fealty. One is blessed.

We do wish Miss Tuttle would make an appearance, at least for civility's sake.

So many years ago, we had tea with mama and father, and Crawfie. What a wonderful woman she was. The soul of service and affection. How time passes, but those memories are fresh. We think the first person who will greet us next, aside from Peter, will be Crawfie. No matter what mama thinks, Crawfie was discreet. We know the truth, with no disrespect to mama, but Crawfie kept her silence those many years, and we communicated with her to reassure her that we held her blameless. Mama means well, forever has. She's in a bit of a fog – who can blame her? A magnificent wife and mother under tremendous hardship, with her chin high and a smile. She and papa led us through the fight. She drinks a bit more than advisable these days. Bless her. But Crawfie was blameless.

How did we go off on that tangent?

Why did we tea alone today? The very day one could benefit from a companion, we're alonesome. Must buck up. We're in a lonely business. So many years here, still, one needs to remember. This seat has room for one. Even Philip, bless him, is an outsider. One is alone, surrounded by everyone and alone.

Miss Tuttle! Miss Tuttle! Where are you? We need you! Miss Tuttle!

No need to raise one's voice. She's here somewhere. Naughty girl. We'd like to see the corgis. Miss Tuttle!

Heavens! We've been in more difficult circumstances. One must remember. We can fix a cracked axle on an American-made jeep in the mud, with a wrench and some baling wire. Now that was a struggle! A missing servant can't top that! Forty-three years like a passing parade. So many, many things. If one person stands out, of all the others we've visited, it is Sālote. A marvel – majestic, warm, honest. Every mite a queen and she was six feet tall! We wish to see her again and sit and talk eye to eye. It will be someday, bless us.

Miss Tuttle! This is absolutely unforgivable! Confound it, where are you?

Martha Hayes was born in October 1894, exact day

unrecorded, to parents who were household domestics for white folks in Richmond, Virginia. At age nineteen, Martha came to New York City as the wife of James Spinnell, four years older than her, an African Methodist Episcopal minister with his church in St. Albans, Queens, and there she raised seven children: four boys and three girls. She was young and innocent, but James was wise, faithful, and patient – and Martha became the same in response. Their marriage found love and respect between them, multiplying over time.

Instead of a church manse, in time Martha and James took a stipend and bought a house in lovely St. Albans, a haven for the black middle class. Their two-story wood-frame home had a small lawn in front and a large garden in back, with apple trees and a vegetable plot for her. She grew kale and collard greens, cucumbers, and onions. The trees provided switches that she used to deliver spankings to her children because she and the reverend believed firmly in "spare the rod, spoil the child." Martha would instruct the errant child to go out back and pick the switch, and woe to the one who brought back a flimsy branch. He or she returned with a sturdy one. In later years, all their sons and daughters gave silent thanks for these ministrations. They were better people as a result of caring, involved parents.

Martha and James had been two people; now they had one life. Through compassion, James smoothed the edges of his stern righteousness. Martha conquered her shyness with the confidence of their total love. Abiding in their devotion, to each other and their family, every day was a sign of this commitment, and every duty a payment of affection. The lessons James taught in church now blossomed into an orchard of precious fruit, children raised in love and care, lives flowering to produce the most magnificent display – a family moving into the future, returning love and care to the world. This was a well-earned success, more valuable than whatever possessions were acquired or money collected. They were often broke financially, but they were not poor. What James and Martha had was implanted into each child. That was immortality on earth. This was riches.

Being church mother, Martha's job was keeping the home for her husband and children, which she did for forty years, seeing them through two world wars, one Great Depression, a cold war, and marriages, broken hearts, hurt feelings, fights, prayers, and small victories. This added up to a full life. She prayed fervently every day. She found herself unselfconsciously humming "I am weak but thou art strong." It was an eternal, not a finite, perspective. She lived the lesson that the less self-involved she was, the more important others in her life became and the more wonderful became her mission with them.

The Reverend Spinnell died in 1960 and the children got married and moved into their own homes and lives, except the youngest son, who was killed in Italy during World War II. Martha displayed her Gold Star as the mother of a fallen soldier for the rest of her life. Soon after her husband passed, she sold her house and moved to Rochdale Village in Queens, an innovative planned community with a targeted 15 percent African-American population. She lived by herself for twenty-six years, self-sufficient and proudly independent.

Going through James's papers during her move, she found an undated note in his hand, apparently written just before his death, regarding its place on his desk on top of the last mortgage payment bills. It read:

My faith is the life in every particle of my being. It is supported by reason and logic, and it stands firm on three pillars. Historically, there is proof Christ lived, taught, and was executed for what He believed. If He had died on Golgotha and didn't return, His followers would have walked away and said that He was another failed prophet. What did happen was they believed even more so, He rose and walked among them, and He fulfilled the prophecies of the Law. If He had died to never return, billions of people wouldn't believe in Him and follow Him today. Scientifically, I look around me and I see life, the earth, and the infinite universe – no man or woman, nothing I know could create this. All this cannot be attributed to an accident. If this is all by chance and without ultimate intelligent design, then I would have to believe that a tornado in a junkyard could produce a fully functioning jet airplane – simply impossible! Finally, my personal experience proves He exists. My prayers are heard and answered – not in my time and way but in His infinite way because He created infinity, He is the Creator of infinity! He lives! The Holy Spirit abides and I will never be alone! He is speaking to me every day.

We all have a longing for God. He created us and gave us free will, but in there, inside of each of us is that longing for Him. How many times have I spoken with atheists and suddenly, involuntarily they come upon a point and say "Thank God!" or "Oh my God!" It's always there, waiting for the spark to set their will on fire and give in to God. The man convinced against his will is of the same opinion still, but let God's will fill you and you're changed forever.

I know this:

At any moment of my life, everything can be taken away, and will be, except my faith – my money, house, health, status, all. No one can remove my faith, though I can try ignorantly to dismiss it.

The government cannot usurp the family, and the family cannot usurp God. Government must support the family and the family must nourish faith. If a child is coddled into adulthood, the child will not know hardship, loss, pain, and failure. But these are the necessary ingredients for maturity. Plant faith in children early and often, and they will grow strong and tall. No man and no government will bend them. No setback will overwhelm them. The big tree with small roots will topple in the breeze, but the small tree with deep roots will endure the storm.

Believe like a child! When my original innocent self is lost, then sin finds me and I find it. If I'm called a child in my old age, it's a compliment. There is my true faith and reliance on my Parent. If I am blessed with old age, I will toddle back to You. My eyes will forsake me, my limbs will go limp, my mind will wander, but You will be there, strong as ever. My Redeemer lives!

She had heard dozens of his sermons, rehearsed at home and delivered on Sundays, though she had not heard him express his thoughts in these words, in this way. Was he defending his faith to an audience of one? She knew him. He was plainspoken; to convince himself was not in him. He was convinced – that's why and how he was a minister of the Word. This note, she was sure, was left for her, a sort of love letter of faith between them, knowing his time here was drawing to a close. It was his testament.

This didn't signal an end – it was an invitation to a new beginning. He knew she would find it at the right time. People in love can plan like that, understanding, feeling, knowing each other intimately. Death has no hold on love. Martha cherished this message in the present, where it was meant to be.

Christ for her and her husband wasn't an abstraction: He was fully human and fully divine.

She kept her husband's note in her handbag and reread it periodically, hearing James's voice and feeling his warm presence. These words sustained her in his corporal absence and moved her in her old age.

By 1987, Martha's physical limitations, especially arthritis, required her, against her will, to have home aides, a reality that broke her spirit and steadily withdrew her grasp of daily life, until three years later when she could not physically leave her home, except by wheelchair. Her daily companion and assistant, Alma Tuttle, stayed with her overnight in the spare bedroom and provided for her needs.

There were days, mostly near the end, when Martha would ask Miss Tuttle, "Please take me home." Miss Tuttle would answer, "You are home," but Martha was undeterred and asked again, "Please take me home." Miss Tuttle, being of uncommon good sense, would get Martha into the wheelchair, walk her outside and around the block, and return home, proudly announcing, "There now, you're home." This happened once a day and was their routine. Martha knew, deep inside, that she wasn't home where she was supposed to be, but she accepted the change of scenery and resolved to go home the next day. She would return to her husband's note. Though her sight was failing, she had memorized it.

On July 4, 1990, Alma suffered a fatal stroke and died on the kitchen floor, though Martha did not know. After drinking her evening tea, Martha tired of calling for Alma with no answer and fell asleep in her favorite chair facing the front window on the first floor of her building. Despairing of the loneliness of the previous day, exhausted, and hearing in her sleep the call of her late husband, Martha peacefully did not awake the following morning. Seeing her slumped in her chair through the window, a passing neighbor called 911. The two bodies were removed in dignity and laid to rest with grace, subsequently.

In the last years of her life, Martha had become fascinated with the British monarchy, the consequence of a vacation she had taken to London, her last trip with her husband, during which he said to her, "You're my queen," a gesture of their love that he repeated continually until his passing. It was his voice, saying that phrase, that she heard on the night of her homegoing.

CHAPTER SIXTEEN

The Shadow in the Valley: A Twisted Tale

Lexington Avenue Subway, Manhattan, March 2, 2006

You don't have a soul. You are a Soul. You have a body.
C. S. Lewis

Thursday

"Do you think she's real or is she a spirit?"

I considered Yael's question and replied, "I don't think I believe in spirits. She's in the flesh all right."

Yael Levi is my dearest friend. He is also the smartest person I know. He speaks six languages plus English. His background includes full scholarship offers from med and law schools and Yale for engineering. Following his own passion, he edits Hebrew publications and writes articles for scientific journals and popular magazines. He is an acknowledged expert in interpreting genetics findings and solving math puzzles. Our friendship spans thirty years, since playing together in the schoolyard at Manhattan's PS 2 on Henry Street. We were known back then as Ebony and Ivory, the basketball twins!

I came to Yael because of recent events of which I was part, in the subways of New York. One subway in particular: the Lexington Avenue line on the East Side, between Grand Central Terminal and East Broadway, every morning from 7:45 through 8:15 a.m. for the last three weeks.

I boarded the downtown Lexington Avenue train at the Grand Central subway station, after my commute south from White Plains, and got off at East Broadway to go to my job as an IT analyst in an office in the gentrified, formerly Jewish Lower East Side.

For three weeks, no matter what car of the train I boarded, across from me sat a woman, the same woman each day. She was nondescript, nothing outstanding or memorable about her. Mundane clothes, expressionless face. Not my type. Dark brown hair, cold blue eyes, trim build, seemingly bored countenance.

When I looked at her, not staring, looking, a female voice, I was convinced it was her voice, entered my head and talked to me. She was looking at me, again not staring but clearly looking at me with a cast on her face that I could best describe being like a fried egg – no emotion or depth.

She said, "You can't help but notice me. Don't look away, I see you. What is it you deeply want to know? Who I am? Is that it? Why me talking to you? How do I always know what car of the train and what seat you'll be in? So many questions and no answers. I know you. I know what's inside you. I've read you for some time, even before you looked at me and noticed. Now, you can't stop, can you?"

This progressed to her saying specific things, although

"progressed" may have been the wrong term. Two weeks ago, I watched her move her left hand deftly into the purse of a young woman seated next to her, who was paying attention to a small boy in a stroller parked in the train's narrow aisle. She, the woman across from me, removed the young woman's wallet and tucked it into a shopping bag, a Henri Bendel shopping bag.

"See that," she said in my brain, "she won't miss it until she's gotten off the train and then it will be too late. There is fifty-seven dollars in it – I don't have to count, I know. All the money she has for the next two days. She needs it for herself and her son. She has no husband, no father at home for the child. I don't need it. I took it because that's what I do, I take. Would you like me to take from you?" Then, I swore, she smiled at me, right at me. Dead at me.

Look, I'm not nuts. I'm a well-grounded, dependable person. Hard worker, love my mom and dad. Dedicated churchgoer. Never in therapy, which I assure you is quite rare for my generation and family circumstances. In fact, I'm the sole person in my circle who hasn't been on the couch, excepting, of course, Yael.

I told Yael this. He was the one I trusted. He listened.

"Don't believe in spirits?" he asked.

"No, I don't."

Yael cocked his head a notch. "You're a Christian. You worship a spirit."

I thought a bit. His logic was unbeatable and I said so. "You're right, but the Holy Spirit, with the definite article, means one spirit, not flocks of spirits roaming the streets."

"Let me tell you something," Yael countered. "My father hasn't worked a legitimate day in his life. Not legitimate from a general point of view. You know we're Orthodox Jews. My dad is the brightest of five sons. He was chosen, and I use that word laden with every possible meaning for the Chosen People, to study Torah forever. He is paid by his community to study Torah seven days a week because studying Torah isn't work. It's love and passion.

"They pay him a living wage to support himself and our family, to read and think Torah, study its minutest inferences and mysteries, and pray. This man, my father, is steeped like a teabag in the spirit. It isn't one spirit or many spirits. It is spirit. In or out of the flesh. Spirit is all around us. It is silently in our everyday lives. For good or evil."

"Yael, I hear you and am trying to understand. But my Savior is holy. Your dad is like a saint. They are about good, not stealing from a poor woman."

Yael looked at me with compassionate eyes. "Ah, my friend. If you believe in the Creator of all things and recognize His Goodness, then you must admit to the opposite. There can be no good without evil. The Creator and Satan, here and now, with the world in the middle."

This was not what I expected to think about at this point.

Yael asked me if there was more to report.

"Yes, unfortunately. Last week, she began saying how she thought about me at night, when she was awake in her bed. Next to her husband! How she can't stop thinking of me. She wants me and furthermore, she knows I want her. In bed. With her. She told me she will have me. 'I will hold you and give you what you deserve' were her words. The next day, she looked at me, then at a middle-aged man seated next to me. She turned back to me and said, 'I will show you what I do.' Not what she could do, but what she does. The man began choking, grabbing his throat, gasping for air, and becoming cyanotic. Somehow, someway she was strangling him to show me."

"What did you do? Did you try to help him?"

What I answered Yael was too strange for me to believe, but I did believe because it happened. "I screamed 'Stop it! Stop it!' reaching out to him in his distress, but looking at her."

"And . . ."

"He stopped choking. He recovered, glared at me, and said, 'Don't yell at me. Can't you see I was in trouble? I couldn't breathe.' It took all of me to tell him I was sorry and didn't mean to yell at him. I couldn't tell him I was yelling at her, that she was doing this to him, as a lark, a prank to impress me. She sat and smiled softly. 'Get it?' she said to me. I had to get off the train before East Broadway and walk ten blocks to the office."

Yael's concern was visible. "What about since then?"

I was ashamed to admit this. "I've been remote from home since that day. Okay, I can do that once or twice but not forever. I've got to go back. I can't bear facing her, hearing her voice in my head. Her taunts and seductions. I don't know what's next. I need your help."

Yael thought for a spell. "You must confront her."

"Yael, impossible. I'll be carted off as a lunatic, a harasser, an attempted rapist! Guilty until proven innocent."

Yael nodded at me and said in a defeated voice, "Yes, you're right. You can't."

We sat together in silence.

"I'll go with you," Yael suggested. "I'll go with you and

look at her. I'll look at her and . . . and I'll pray. Yes, that's it, I'll pray. Maybe that's the strongest weapon. I'll look at her and pray the Shema. The prayer of my people. What we pray when we are alone or in danger or need."

I can't say he convinced me, but I didn't have a better plan.

Friday

I met Yael under the clock in Grand Central.

"You know," I told l him, "this clock isn't made of mother-of-pearl. The value is due to it being the world's largest clock made of brass and opal glass." I was nervous and attempting to lighten the mood. This failed.

"I usually appreciate trivia but today of all days, we must focus. If we're right, we're facing an evil spirit. We cannot do this lightly."

He was right. At least, I thought he was.

I took him along and randomly waited at the middle of the platform. It didn't matter: she would be there, wherever I sat.

So it was. We boarded and there she was. For the first time, she diverted her look from me to someone else, Yael. Because his family was Yemenite Jews, he wore his *tallit* throughout the day, with the fringes, the *tzitzit* showing from under his jacket. On his head was his *kippah*. No mistaking that Yael was a Jew and sundown was Shabbat.

I stared at her forcefully and openly, thinking the Twenty-Third Psalm, "The Lord is my Shepherd . . ." Yael was reciting the Shema in an undertone, "Shema Yis-rael . . ."

Her words came rushing to my head, spilling over each other with hatred and venom. "A filthy Jew! You bring this Jew to me, brazenly in all his Jewishness! You make me sick. You want to spurn me for this pig? How dare you. I know him. I know his *davening* father, that fat Jew. Get away! Get away!"

But I was not the one getting away and neither was Yael. She leapt from her seat, pushed and shoved all out of her way, and forced the train doors open. Yael and I saw her standing on the platform, her eyes red like hell's flames, as the moving train passed.

I leaned back in my seat and Yael put his hand on my shoulder. He whispered, full of satisfaction, "We did it! We overcame her. You won't see her again."

I was weary and wary. "Are you sure? Are you totally sure?"

"No, not totally. That was evil, the devil, Satan's messenger. The Creator's foulest enemy. I don't speak out of turn. The seducer who wanted you."

"Me? Why?"

"Not your body, my friend. Your soul. Satan needs souls for his gang, souls like that creature we chased. In the New Testament, Satan tempted Christ directly. Satan doesn't have any power over you, the Holy One does. Satan is a deceiver, who tries to trick you. Satan has no spiritual power, just our own shame, greed, and hatred. He uses us against ourselves when we allow him. That's why he enlists slaves to do his bidding and lay traps for you and me. It's your choice, free will, to be ensnared by it or resist. The difference is faith."

I was relieved and horrified at once. We thought it was over.

Saturday

Yael and I sat at the table in his family's Borough Park, Brooklyn, home.

We were brunching on bagels, nova, cream cheese, sliced onions, and capers. Yael's father was aware of what occurred the previous day. Rather than being skeptical, he was contemplative. "If that was a seducing demon, Lilith, you fought, then prayer was the weapon of choice. I take it as a badge of honor to be ridiculed. I am a Jew, I do *daven*, and I am fat. Remember, Satan has been trying to kill the Jews since the day Moses declared there was one God." We didn't speak of it at the table anymore. I felt safe and loved in this company, like I did in my own home and with my own church family.

Sunday

The front page of the Sunday *New York Post* screamed a bloody headline: "Subway Rider Murdered on the #4 Tracks." The accompanying story was chilling. Eyewitnesses saw an obviously enraged woman shove a young man onto the tracks of an incoming southbound 4 train. Then, she disappeared into the crowd.

Reading this, a nauseous wave swept over me. The evil had not been banished.

CHAPTER SEVENTEEN

The Army of the Forgiven

Riverdale, The Bronx, July 18, 2018

*As you reach each window, an unknown hand opens it
and the light it lets in only increases by contrast the
darkness of the end of the passage.*
Sir Winston Churchill

My analyst corrected me when I said my family was normal.

"All families are abusive; it's a question of how. Adler said the only normal people are the ones you don't know very well."

I saw him because I was having bad dreams. One in particular about my dad. Not exactly about him, but with him. Dad looked at me, not saying a word. I think his eyes were pleading with me or crying, I couldn't figure which. He was dead six years now and he kept turning up in my dreams. The same dream, over and over.

"It's common for women to dream about their fathers, especially fathers who are gone," my analyst responded when I told him. I wasn't interested in what was common. This was *my* problem and it was *my* dad visiting *me* in *my* sleep.

I suppose a dream is a small thing. Have it, wake up, go on with life, fall asleep, press rewind. After many reruns, I felt like that TV detective – it's the little things that bother me. I was at that point when this had to stop. My dream was hanging on and wrecking my whole day. I wanted my memories of my dead dad to leave me alone.

My relationship with my dad growing up was best described as "of course I loved him, but . . ." He loved me; I knew that. He could also be a loudmouth wiseass, thoroughly convinced of his own infallibility and everyone must be likewise convinced. He was embarrassing. He didn't know when to shut up. I hid in my skin the minute he opened his mouth in public.

He provided for us, my mom and me, and worked like a dog to give us the comforts of a middle-class life. He sacrificed having his own extras, like a new car every so often and new clothes and his beloved steak for special dinner, to buy us a house in Riverdale so I could go to an expensive school, Moral Culture Academy, and have a big green lawn in the city. I did love him for that. He sat with me when I was sick and went to work late if I had a doctor's appointment because he absolutely needed to be sure I was well and healthy. I caught him crying one night when I was ten, heartsick that I had the flu, and blaming himself that he didn't do enough to protect me from nature's illnesses. I had to honor his sacrifice.

Why then was I still bitter at him for being a jerk?

"You say your father was a jerk. Is that because you felt embarrassed about him, about his . . . outspokenness?"

"He made me cringe, saying stupid things . . ."

"Like?"

"Stupid things like he knew medicine better than the

doctors. Like he didn't have to go to school to know how to treat sickness. Like he talked over people, he'd shout them down. Like he couldn't listen without talking down to everybody. He was obnoxious."

"He's dead."

"Yeah, he's dead."

"Do you miss him?"

No, I didn't think I did, but hearing that question I choked up. I was going to cry. Having run him down to my analyst, I suddenly was confronted by the fact that my dad was my loving parent, no matter how embarrassing he could be. I did love him and I missed him now and he was reappearing in my dreams as if he wanted my forgiveness. Could I forgive him?

I shook my head no but I answered, "Yes, I miss him. He loved me. He took care of me. He was better at that than my mom. I sometimes think he could be so infuriating because my mom was so cold. And dumb. She was dumb, she had no other way to be. She was unaware of the world around her. She never saw the world, just her nails and her hair."

"She was self-absorbed?"

That wasn't the right word. "She was self-centered. While dad was crying over my illness, she was picking out what dress to wear the next day. What dress to wear! She wasn't going anywhere. She was a stay-at-home housewife and goodness knows she didn't do much housework. Our housekeeper, Mrs. O'Keefe, did the housework. Mom smoked cigarettes and drank cocktails, as if she was born to live in Riverdale with the swells. She was no swell. She was Kitty Jablonski from East Harlem, who lucked into marrying Jed Goldman, who broke his back for her. And me."

Where did all of that come from, I wondered, years and years after my mom retired from never working and perched herself on the sofa in our living room, waiting to kiss dad on his cheek when he got home from being a wage slave and then supervising Mrs. O'Keefe's preparation of dinner? I almost never thought about my mom. She was a supporting player in the drama starring dad and me. Why wasn't I dreaming about her instead of dad? Should I forgive her?

"This is new material." To my analyst my inner turmoil was material. "Our session is over. I will see you next Tuesday."

Ending my sessions was an unsatisfying conclusion. I knew I was done, but was that all there was? For two hundred fifty dollars cash and wait for the insurance reimbursement, see you next week?

I made my way crosstown to my office having spent my lunch hour on the fifty-minute, once-a-week appointment.

I was off the bus heading to the office building. Instinctively I reached for my office keys. Not in my jacket pocket. Not in my pants pocket. Not in my briefcase. I went through the progression again. Dammit, my keys! Was it going to be one of those days?

"Miss?"

I turned around at the sound of that antiquated word directed at me. Miss who?

"Are these yours?" The older man extended his hand to me, holding my key chain.

"Yes? Yes! Oh please, thank you. Thank you. I thought I lost them. Thank –"

"No worries." He actually tipped his driving cap to me. Old man manners.

Saved from the embarrassment of asking the custodian to let me into my own office, I smiled to start the second part of my workday. I was on autopilot, moved paper from one side of my desk to the other, shuffled numbers in spreadsheets, and answered telephone calls with "hey," "yes," "okay," and "sure, thanks." All the time thinking about my session. Thoughts of my mom and dad flooded over me with memories of their faces playing on that screen in my mind. Their photo was on my desk, with my dad in his trademark wool cap and my mom with her hands on his shoulders. Two people, both dead, first her then him, and their faces bouncing back and forth inside of me. For years they were my world, my closeted world. What I saw and lived was filtered through them.

I wasn't them on purpose. I was warm, unlike my mom, and quiet, unlike my dad. I didn't want kids unlike both of them. They both had to leave me be. That's the way life was supposed to be. They were gone and I was alive.

On my uptown subway ride home, I blocked thoughts of them to focus on my aim for the rest of the day – a good night's sleep and no parental visitations. My plan was a predinner drink, Campari and tonic; a warm meal, scratch macaroni and white cheddar cheese; a long, hot shower; and decaf green tea in my large mug while curled up in my reclining chair sewing.

I inherited Mrs. O'Keefe's sewing box, an old-fashioned red, green, and gold tin that once held a Christmas fruitcake. In it were the needles, pins, thimbles, spools of thread, and haphazard patches of cloth our housekeeper employed to darn socks and hem dresses for me. I sewed not to repair my clothes now but to busy my hands while I relaxed. I found a forest-green square of cotton and remembered how warmly content I could be when I was young. That green square was from my lightweight blanket. The memory wasn't one particular time or place. It was the all too real sensation of a long ago feeling that once covered me.

Tucked under my current comforter, I said a thank-you out loud to a Creator my father talked about, One I didn't see. One I didn't talk to often enough. I remembered my dad's words, "It's more important to listen than to ask," a notion he seldom applied to himself, I thought. Lately, I neither listened nor asked, tending to let my life move onward without much thought. That night, I prayed for a resolved sleep, like the sleep I experienced when all was well and I was a child in my own bed, under my forest-green cotton blanket.

I awoke the next morning more refreshed than I could remember recently, and I quizzed myself about what, if anything, I dreamt the previous night. It sat in the back of my mind. It was there, but not in a form I could describe. I couldn't put words to it easily. I did dream. The memory of having dreamt was so bright it glowed, but what was it? After thirty seconds awake, the normal memory of a dream tended to evaporate.

I poured a cup of coffee. The dream materialized as I looked into the cup. Dad drank a single cup of coffee every morning. He was in the dream, wearing his driving cap: this time he smiled like he and I were sitting together in our Riverdale home. Mom was standing behind him, smiling with her hands lovingly on his shoulders. They were so much in love and they loved me. They told me they loved me.

Although their lips didn't move, they spoke in unison. "We did our best. It's not perfect; it's our love. Our love makes mistakes. We give what we have. Now you do the same. Don't be us. Be you. We made a family because we weren't perfect. We were a lesson; now you be the lesson. We're all here. Our lives were important for what we gave you – a man with us here, number 42 starting at second base for Brooklyn, taught us that. Someday you will say the same. You'll be a soldier in the army and have the strength to forgive. We forgive and become forgiven. No worries, dear daughter, you're loved."

In my sleep, I hugged them. They had always been there, deep inside and with me. They were always more than just characters in my life. They were my parents.

I gave sincere thanks for my problem. It took me back to them. It showed me their grace; not a cheap grace that, like shoe polish, wears off in time, but a true one that endures and deepens naturally with age. Their love for me outshone their frail humanity. They wanted me to know their love was alive. It outlived death. It lived in me. A life without the love of both parents is, at best, a half-lived life. I understood – how do I know the strength and power I possess, through love, if I'm not tested? I could not see the light without passing through the darkness. The summit is only reached climbing uphill. Fear not, love is with me.

Were all my problems solved in an instant? Of course not. Life is always harder than that. But I realized for the first time that my mother tried her best at what she knew – being loyal and loving to my father. He did what he could, in the best way he knew how, to love and serve his family. What I did repair was my affection and honor for them both, broken people, as all of us are broken and flawed. They had lived for me, and their love had carried me to my present. To forgive and accept them was to do the same for myself. I was full of faults and contradictions: to expect my parents or anyone to be perfect was cruel and ignorant.

So many people angry that others weren't so perfect like they thought themselves to be. I wasn't going to be one of them. I made my choice based on love, not the cancers of jealousy and anger. I still had issues to address, but I was on my way, on firm ground. I resolved to breathe free air and dispel the poison of blame. I wasn't going to choke on the past and its grudges. Something I was taught in my fancy private school was reminded to me. I must not be, I would not be, King Lear's thankless child, as sharp as a serpent's tooth. I would listen to the king's court jester in the storm because the jester whispered to me – forgive.

Upon entering my office that day, I triumphantly dialed my analyst's phone number and got the answering service.

"This is Helen Goldman. Thank you. I'm canceling my appointment next week and forever. I found my material."

CHAPTER EIGHTEEN

Loaves of Bread

Howard Beach, Queens, March 10, 1979

No legacy is so rich as honesty.
William Shakespeare

My mother and father got out with their lives. They made it out alive but wounded: deeply wounded in their souls, and they passed those wounds on to me.

They told me Vienna, what they called Wein, was a pretty place, filled with gardens and music, overflowing with pastries and hungry scholars. It was the cultural center of Austria. A place where geniuses gathered to write and expound their learned theories. Where musicians wrote and played the most divine songs. And people drank their lives away while dancing. The home and host to Beethoven, Freud, Strauss, Klimt, and Kafka. I remembered precious little of that lovely place. I did remember the ugliness, though. That, I wouldn't forget.

All this ended in March 1938. From July 1934 to then, the lit fuse on the German time bomb for Austria sizzled, and finally exploded. My parents weren't alone in knowing the SS had infiltrated Vienna since 1934 – their agents were as noticeable as wiggling worms in a bowl of porridge. The Nazis annexed a willing Austria, with the Wehrmacht being greeted by German-worshipping Austrians of a certain background, pathetic boys lusting for adventure and heroic blood, and girls with open legs. I can still hear the bells pealing from everywhere – bells welcoming the Nazis into Vienna, triumphant bells to hail the new order. The world would now be put right. The enemies of divine destiny would be hounded and rioted out of existence. German life mattered, again. The satanic Hitler arrived as conqueror in April and fatso Göring followed in May. They were worshipped. People licked their smelly feet.

My parents were Sephardic and deeply atheist. Their ancestors came to Austria from Syria, intending to move westward, but they stopped in that beautiful place and settled instead. For them, religion, all religion was a monumental waste of time, a hollow joke on those gullible enough to believe. We held ourselves above the Ashkenazi babblers and scrappers, fawning over a mirage. It's impossible to believe that one benevolent universal intelligence created both the Nazis and me.

After the Anschluss, my parents knew what came next. They had seen this twenty years earlier when sixty thousand French and Belgians were carted off to concentration camps as hostages of the Krauts, and they knew about the siege of Lille, France. The Jews fleeing Russian pogroms came west, to Germany, Russia's foe in the war. But the Germans, with their proclivity for precision, counted the incoming Jews, photographed them, and gave them identification documents. The Jews were herded into railway cars to be deloused before entry. Sound familiar? It was to my parents. It was our turn. The Germans didn't change. Germans, Gummiehals, Boche, Bazi, Boxheads, Krauts, Huns, Heinies, Jerrys, Piefke – the name wasn't important. They were what they were.

If culture is shared understanding and values, then the Germans weren't members of the same species that I was. They didn't belong to humanity.

Our maid, a Christian girl, disappeared. Whether she no longer wanted to be in our household or she was coerced to leave, I only know one day shortly after the Nazis arrived, she was gone and never seen again. She didn't collect her final pay packet: it sat untouched on a bureau in the front hall for a week, until mother opened it and put the money in her pocket. By then we suspected we would need it more than the maid. The privileges of success were gone.

The next day there came the expected and dreaded knock at the door. The SS, in plain clothes and out in the open now, inventoried our artwork to satisfy the Nazi lust, and seized my mother's jewelry. That was only the start.

The Vienna gas company ceased supplying Jewish homes to try to stop the flood of Jews who were committing suicide. Several of our neighbors jumped from their balconies.

Our family business, *Kleine Konditorei,* an elegant confectionery shop that catered to the famous Viennese sweet tooth, was ransacked, burned, and forbidden to reopen. My father was taken away to the hastily constructed concentration camp at Vienna's northwest rail station. I witnessed an elderly man with a scraggly white beard being knocked to the ground by a group of kids who had been my playmates. They kicked and spat on him and stole his fur hat, like a brutal child's game of cops and robbers in reverse. I saw other things done to women I don't talk about. People I thought I knew were unrecognizable. They became monsters, the likes of which I had never seen before. I was not permitted to attend school anymore, where I excelled in my studies and had lots of friends. That was all gone in a blinding flash – no school, no studying, and no friends. The last word was, I was a Jew, not a boy or a classmate or a friend. A dirty Jew. I was cast out and passed over. Everywhere, the sidewalks were spotted red. Men were horsewhipped in broad daylight, surrounded by cheering crowds. I was caught in a blur where the real and the fictional merged: imagined horror became a daily sight. I blotted most of this from my memory, but not all. I vowed I would never be kicked without kicking back twice as hard. Weakness is death.

My mother, the clever one in the family, walked to the makeshift camp defiantly and bribed my father out. The Austrian Nazis were pigs, but greedy pigs. The Austrian shilling was backed by four times the amount of gold as the reichsmark, and my mother had a bagful of shillings for the pigs to look the other way while my father strolled out, hand in hand with her. We planned our escape and saved what money we could. Using what we had left, mother prepared passage for me, their one child and son, and my cousin Edvard to transit to France and then on to America. My parents, my aunt and uncle, and the other family would join us soon after: they figured a large Jewish family traveling together might trigger Nazi suspicions and wreck our plans.

Edvard and I sailed on a freighter on the rocky North

Atlantic, all the passengers vomiting day and night. A Swedish sailor took pity on us two boys and told us "eat potatoes and you'll be fine." We did and landed in America at Ellis Island. Except for our parents, our relatives young and old were killed in the camps. I had photos of many of them, but I didn't remember who they were. I found it difficult to believe they ever existed. They were erased. Memory is funny that way – what's most painful is locked out of mind, though lingering disturbingly deep within, like a knot in my belly.

The American hero, President Roosevelt, wouldn't allow Jews fleeing Hitler to enter the US to stay. He didn't want to betray America's neutrality before going to war. He turned a ship full of fleeing Jews back around, to return to Nazi Germany and be exterminated. One of my cousins, Albere, was a doomed passenger. I wondered why, when I learned that New York Mayor La Guardia in 1934 had spoken publicly about Germany's determination to slaughter the Jews, Roosevelt didn't utter a word. To prove La Guardia stood for his beliefs, in 1938 after Kristallnacht, he put a police guard in front of the German consulate with twelve Jewish officers commanded by Captain Finkelstein! Roosevelt did nothing. After Roosevelt died, Americans built statues to him and I shook my head.

We were lucky to be diverted to Cuba, where we had family who accepted us temporarily. A month later, we were joined there by our parents. In Havana, we lived like royalty, eating tropical fruit, learning to speak Spanish, and being waited on by servants, who were poor, beleaguered Cubans, happy to earn a good living being maids and cooks. In short order after Pearl Harbor, our American cousins were able to take us all into their home in Queens, New York.

I left Cuba a seventeen-year-old, transplanted from German-speaking Vienna, where I had learned English as well, to Spanish-speaking Havana, to Queens as an American. Almost three years later, I was a US Army private stationed in the Pacific, an engineer fighting to take islands and atolls from the Imperial Japanese forces, and proud to be in the action. Upon entering the military, I was granted citizenship.

Here I was, an immigrant Austrian boy, and instead of killing Germans, I was mopping up the leftover Japanese soldiers as the US marched across the Pacific aiming at Japan. It felt odd fighting these soldiers in the tropics; they knew they were coming to a fatal end, and we knew they weren't about to surrender. It was in their blood to not be captured alive, an utter humiliation to their nation, family, and ancestors in the beyond. The ones we did take prisoner involuntarily defecated and wet their ragged shorts on the spot; it was embarrassing to have to stand there, them at gunpoint, and watch this. They thought we were going to do to them what they were drilled to do to us if the roles were reversed. They were strange buggers, with a fixed look like they were staring into eternity. We captured a few dozen, maybe not that many, during months of island hopping. I would rather have killed all of them instead of caring for this subhuman filth.

The ones that fought battled to their last fingernail. We would land on an island with superior force, set base, conduct reconnaissance, and map the targets. Then we surrounded the bunker, hole in the ground, cave, or pile of rocks and called to them to give up and no harm would be done. This was always answered by a round of gunfire from them or a mortar – they didn't have much firepower left, but they used what they had and aimed to kill. We wasted no time at this little game. Out came the portable flamethrowers, that were my responsibility to prepare and fuel. Full of fuel, they weighed seventy pounds. Firing one of these in the heat of the tropics is no small job. Do it wrong and you get burned. It was good for seven seconds and that was all we needed. A few blasts into the intended place and the stench of barbequed human flesh and the screams were an unforgettable experience. The handful of POWs removed the remains and burnt survivors at the end of our assaults. To them, it was an honor. Left up to me, I would have spit on what was left.

The incongruity wasn't lost on me that on the other side of the globe, most of my relatives had already been through the same thing. If I couldn't do it to the Germans, I was happy to do it to their allies. My relatives weren't given the opportunity to surrender. I could have cared less about these professional soldiers who clung to their masturbatory dreams of glory in death. I will give them this though: they valued death with their crazed sense of honor over living as whimpering, beaten dogs.

I was preparing my gear to ship out as one of the first Americans headed for the invasion of Japan when I received word of Hiroshima, and then Nagasaki. For the rest of my life, I chuckled quietly whenever I heard some American eggheaded liberal argue about the immorality of dropping those bombs. Buddy, you should have been in my shoes. If I could have dropped one on the Nazis, I would have considered it a pleasure. Every roasted German would have been another step toward peace. It would have been a kindness; they were already dead from the neck up.

The fewer Germans left standing to piss against a wall, the better.

Immediately after the Nazis surrendered and the Russians ruled post-war Berlin, the former Hitler Youth leaders quickly became the Anti-Fascist youth leaders for the conquered Germans. The former Nazi Party members and their adult children were conscripted to clean up the rubble from the bombings. Many of them worked up to sixteen hours per day. Their reaction? "Why must we be humiliated?" What did I say before? Sorry only for themselves, they remained the same.

I made my way in the world. I told myself, no loving deity would allow to happen what happened in Europe in my childhood. My parents weren't religious. I was forsaking something I had never known anyway. My cousin Edvard and his parents were deeply religious. He and I studiously avoided discussing that topic. The nearest we came was at a dinner in our home in Jackson Heights, Queens, shortly after I gained my citizenship and before I shipped out. The family got to talking about the last days in Vienna. My mother remarked, "Did God abandon us?" which was a rhetorical question on her part because she didn't believe in God. Edvard replied, "Maybe we abandoned God," and he meant it. I looked at them both and said, "Maybe we abandoned ourselves," and I was being honest. Edvard responded, "We let the Romans burn the temple." He had studied in Hebrew school. Discussion ended.

Life for me was a practical, not a spiritual, matter. I've done things I'm still not proud of, but I survived and answered to myself. I hung out with people who did their own business and spoke a lot of Italian and some Yiddish.

Not being Ashkenazi, I never picked up the Yiddish (what my parents called "bastardized German, a language of poetry mangled by ignorant peasants"), but I sure learned Italian quickly, so I could hold my own in working with my acquaintances.

In 1979, I was given an opportunity to help my friends and make some serious bread. My sometimes partner Guido told me to go to the races.

Guido's nickname was the Horse. He was a born horse-player. He bet the horses, including the trotters (what the Italians call *trotto*) at Yonkers and Roosevelt Raceways, which was like betting on a merry-go-round, it was so fixed. He did whatever he had to do to get money for betting on the ponies. He wasn't your typical hooked gambler because he provided for his family, and his kids were never in the streets without a home and milk. But he lived for playing the horses. I would say he was a one-man Off-Track Betting parlor, in front of and behind the betting window. He always wore a porkpie hat. He and I were absolutely straight with each other.

I met Guido at the Big A, Aqueduct Racetrack, near the $100 ticket windows, and we chatted. He's got on his signature flattop hat, like that famous architect. First thing he tells me is someone from another business crew wants to see me.

"For what?" I ask.

"He says he has a deal."

"So, why can't he come to me himself?"

"He thinks you don't like him."

Who is this, a teenager? I asked myself.

"Who?"

"That pizza face with the spoon up his nose, works out

of JFK. The airport thing. Ah-Ah."

He was saying the Italian word for the letter *A,* twice. A-A. I knew who it was.

The airport thing was five million dollars stolen from a secure hangar and every crook knew who did it, but the cops had a stick up their ass looking for it. Now I know who wants to see me. He was a junkie and a known crook.

"Okay. You friendly with him?" I would be surprised if Guido hung around a person like this.

"No. He knows I know you and he has something to propose to you."

"A deal, not a beef?"

"A deal, yeah. I wouldn't carry a beef from him to anyone I know."

That was the right answer for me.

"Look, I'd talk to J. Edgar Hoover himself if he had a good deal. Tell him to meet me at the club where I hang out, tomorrow afternoon. I don't want to be seen with him after dark."

"Will do."

The junkie meets me in the early afternoon. I'm thinking maybe this is the best time for him because later in the day he'll have so much coke up his nose, he won't be able to talk straight. I look at him and am reminded why he is such a loser. He is a dog in church, Italians say *un cane in chiesa*, an unwelcome guest. He is a dog, a dirty dog. I dislike him intensely. He's too much of a loser for me to waste my time hating. Being on junk is a sickness. Nazis I hate; junkies I keep at a distance.

His clothes are rumpled and his hair is greasy. He looks like he hasn't taken a bath in a couple of days, and for sure he hasn't shaved. Why would anyone trust him to make a deal? Because he was always around money, like a fly on a golden turd.

He greets me, "Hey, we met once before."

I'm looking at him and haven't convinced myself that he is worth talking to. "Yeah. You want me for something?"

He doesn't care that I'm being rude. I certainly didn't care – a donkey drinking from a bottle had better manners than him.

"Yeah. Yeah. I got something we can make some serious *scarole*." *Scarole* is Italian for many escaroles, endives, greens – money, lots of money.

"What are we talking?" Serious has a number of meanings.

"How about a million?"

"How about it?"

"How about you seeing your Jew friend in Florida and turning a million easy."

"How easy?"

"Easy. You know the Jew."

This is all funny because I happen to know this junkie is married to a Jew, a sweet girl from Long Island he turned into a coke addict, and that by birth I'm a Jew. Meaningless to the junkie.

"I know lots of people. Some of them are Jewish. Most of them are good people. What do you want from my friend?"

"Hey, buddy, this is no game. I'm letting you work on a million bucks. All you got to do is clean it up and take a slice. Easy money."

"I tell you what. Why don't we go to the office in the back and you lay it all out for me."

In the office he tells me the story. A chunk of that

airport thing was a million dollars in bearer bonds. With bearer bonds, all you have to do is present them to the bank and you get the cash. There aren't any ownership records. That's why nobody issues them nowadays: too ripe for theft. They're totally liquid, except in this case, a million dollars' worth at one time would ring a lot of bells. The cops haven't mentioned it because they don't want to tip off the thieves that they know about the bonds. Then, maybe if the cops get lucky, the thieves will present the bonds and give themselves away. The junkie and his friends need to get the bonds to my Florida friend and take a percentage on the dollar without exposing their position. Nice, easy work if I want it. A million in my hands, I want.

I tell the junkie, "I'll think about it and get back to you."

Like most druggies, he doesn't register emotion one way or another. A million dollars couldn't wake him up from his coke heaven. Pathetic waste of human life. But a million is a million. I'm sure he has possession of it, and he and his partners have to get rid of it pronto. That puts me in a good position.

I got back to him the next day, through Guido, and told him to hold tight, I'd trade in his bonds. Guido brought the bonds to me. I drove down to Florida alone. This was my deal. My friend was selective about who he dealt with.

My friend picked up the phone on the third ring and recognized my voice. "Hello, young fella. It's been a while." He never used my name on the phone. I was always "young fella." Never mind I was in my fifties. He was in his eighties. "Yes, sir. I'd like to drop by. I got some rye bread from Katz's. The kind you like with no seeds."

"Oh! You're so kind. How many?"

"Ten loaves." A loaf was a hundred thousand dollars.

He dealt in large loaves.

"Ten. That's generous. I always welcome visitors." He gave me an address on North Flagler Drive in West Palm Beach that was not his home. I looked it up on the map in my glove compartment.

When I arrived, I saw that it was an Orthodox Jewish synagogue, with a white plaster facade. A directory in the front said, "A jewel of a shul!" Standing next to the directory was my friend, wearing blue- and white-striped seersucker pants, a short-sleeve white shirt that looked starched, and canvas shoes. He wore a yarmulke, something he hadn't worn when I last saw him at his home.

"You look well. Come in from this heat." He was the host and not a drop of perspiration on him. I admired how cool he was, inside and out.

I carried my bag. We entered. It was a large, airy building with a lobby that branched off to several hallways and doors. The tall ceiling was wood, cypress I think, and the floors were cedar planks. It was an impressive building.

"Come, sit." He beckoned me with a short wave of his hand into the sanctuary. It must have sat four hundred people when full. I followed him up a flight of stairs to the balcony. There were plenty of seats there too, but the whole place was vacant. On the balcony front rail was a half-height wall of glass, clear on our side.

He motioned me to sit.

"This is the part where the women sit. It's called the *mechitza*, the division. We do this so there is no intermingling of the sexes during prayer and no impure temptation. This is so that all remain serious. It protects the dignity of both the men and the women. The other side of this glass is opaque."

I put the bag on the seat between us.

Sitting there, he fit in this place. He belonged here as much he belonged anywhere.

He looked at me quietly with his youthful eyes. His face showed his age, but not his eyes. They were clear and bright, full of life and curiosity.

It took several moments before he spoke.

"I hope you don't mind meeting here."

"Not at all." I had no notion of what a synagogue was like, having never been in one, as far as I remembered.

"It's not really a church, you know. Not really a church. For us, the church is in our hearts when ten men meet. This is a *shul,* or school. We learn here and we also pray here, but this is not like a church." He knew I was born a Jew and that I had zero Jewish upbringing. My atheist parents did not attend synagogue. They saw synagogues as mumbo-jumbo palaces. They never set foot in a synagogue, at least not that I could recall. I wasn't even circumcised. In these matters, I was blank like a Christian. Five years earlier, I had read a book and learned the famous Robert Moses had been raised by his parents the same way, not even circumcised. Imagine that, and his family name was Moses!

"It's okay to talk business here?" I asked.

"Business is part of life. There is no separation. I give money to this *shul*; money makes this possible. We must live our lives and provide for our loved ones. Besides, no one will overhear us here."

Okay by him, okay by me.

He looked at me again in a studious way, as if through

my skin.

"I know that you are trusted by many important people."

It was a statement, not a question. I stayed silent. That trust brought me to him.

"You are honest and hardworking. These are admirable traits. This is supposed to come with years, but that doesn't happen enough nowadays. I know many lazy old fools. Success is a habit, you know."

He was reading me.

"I liked your friend very much." He was talking about a recently departed mutual friend, shot dead in the prime of his life. Killed by his business associates. "Vanity is a sin. It strikes the high and the lowly. Don't take me incorrectly. I am not the judge of sinners, being one myself. I am one man. But I can see fatal blindness in my fellow man. A tremendous loss. That was a good man, an honest man. A friend. Blind, in the end. A pity. His eyes were darkened and he could not see and his back was bent. Had I known him better I would have warned him not to live behind a wall, separated from reality. You cannot live your life not seeing or knowing how others see you. You have to see from the inside out and from within, in order to survive and prosper. You must see yourself through the eyes of others. You have to know how you are seen or you are sightless. A shrewd man observed, 'Worse than being blind is to not want to see.'"

I think I understood what he was saying.

He looked at me and then at my hands. He knew the things I had done so far. He was a kindly old man staring at me. I was to him a little boy. He smiled.

"I want to give you some advice. Something more

valuable than our business deal. My advice, young fella, is for you to always know the difference between those pieces of paper in your bag and your life. Those pieces of paper with numbers and words have no destiny. Quite soon they will be worthless. You have a destiny. What you are truly worth is up to you. Don't be the person who lives his life and dies a fool."

He turned slowly to gaze at the bag. There was a ray of sunshine coming from a side window and landing directly on us, shining like we were on fire.

"Now, tell me about what you've brought." We were down to business.

"I'm representing these for someone else. They need to be liquid."

"Yes, liquid is the best. You say ten loaves?"

"Yes."

"May I examine the produce?"

He leaned over and peered inside the bag, then took out one bundle of bonds. His eyes were so clear that if you saw them, you'd say he was twenty years old. He looked at the stack of paper the way you might look at a carton of eggs in the supermarket to see if any were cracked, smiled again, and commented, "Good."

He touched a few of the bonds gently, then he straightened up and said, "All good. The genuine article. At this time there is but one way you could bring this to me. That airport business. A bold move, but I know you were not involved."

He paused.

"Yes, you are now the holder in due course. Innocent of anything else that has touched these. I can guess who is the original party. Something of a disappointment because

I would much rather be doing business with you directly. So be it. You and I are aware that there is a dogged pursuit for the original party, through these bonds."

"I know," I confirmed.

"That means we cannot negotiate these openly like we did last time with what you brought. At least not in the United States. These will take more effort; however, there are investors in other parts who are eager to include these in their portfolios for the long term and a rainy day." Bearer bonds were not traceable. Time, patience, and a discount would make these clean.

He was silent, and then he excused himself and walked down the stairs. I sat and waited, thinking about him and what he had said. I didn't count time. The room was quiet and calm, but it was also formal and stiff. It wasn't inviting. Apart from my business, I wasn't welcomed here. I guessed it was populated by people unlike my aunts and uncles, who got out in time. After a bit, he returned carrying two brown paper shopping bags with the words "Rascal House" printed on their sides.

"I will give the party you represent sixty cents on the dollar, out of which I will retain a five cents per handling fee. I leave it to you how you deliver this."

I was going to take a healthy cut and he knew it.

He patiently set down his bags on the floor between us and moved my bag to the chair on his right. Our business was done. He had $550,000 in cash nearby, probably in his car. Now he had one million dollars in bearer bonds. I imagined how much this old man had stashed in his home. Millions. Who knew? He was fearless.

"It has been a distinct pleasure for me to spend this time with you. You are good company." With that, he rose from his seat. "If you will pardon me, it is time for me to go home and enjoy my siesta. When you are ready, you may let yourself out of here, the doors are open. This is a public place. There is no hurry. You are welcome to stay as you wish."

We had transacted one and a half million dollars of business in a public place. Under the nose of the Jewish Lord.

He extended his hand. I looked at it: boney, big knuckles, and blue veins, with liver spots. His grip was firm; he was no old weakling. I was sure if need be, he could defend himself bravely. He walked down the stairs and was gone.

I took a few minutes to look around. I did not fit there. I drove back to Queens.

I now wanted to be done with this deal quickly. I told Guido to bring the junkie back to the club in the late afternoon and stick around. I guessed I might need a witness.

The junkie looked like he hadn't bathed or shaved since I last saw him, but he was wearing different clothes. Different, not cleaner. A junkie never changes. He is one thing, and one thing only. I'm amazed at how some of them hang on to life. The human body can withstand a ton of punishment for incredibly long before falling apart. Death is standing right next to them and they keep resolutely climbing into the grave, step by step. They didn't have to be nudged.

I gave him no greeting, no pleasantries. Somehow what my old friend had said to me made me even angrier at doing a deal with this human waste.

"Look. I got fifty cents on the dollar. Take it or leave

it."

"Fifty cents? On a mil? That's no good. I can't go back with that. I hear you got sixty cents last year on a bundle. I can't take this."

He was looking to skim a slice right off the top; now he had less wiggle room with the cash. I knew what he was about. I had no mercy for him.

"What I got or didn't get isn't your concern. You don't spend my money."

"A mil! You can do better. You know who I'm with."

This dirt bag was twisting my horns. This coked-up junkie. I had enough.

"I'm going to give you your paper back. Get out of here. You take your paper and get pinched. Then you can go back to selling junk in the can with your scumbag buddies. There is no business between us."

I'm seeing if he is a man, or does he fold?

A few seconds elapse.

He folds.

"Hey, let's do business. Why are we arguing? Okay? Fifty cents works. It works. I'd like more but it works. I'm not here to fight. If it was forty cents I took back, my people would think you screwed them."

Especially if he was the one who took a hundred grand off the top before giving his crew the dough. I'd make a big, fat target. A junkie will double-cross his mother for a lot less. This one would peddle her ass on the street for the next fix.

"You're not so sharp. Screwed them? You walk out of here with this bag and tell them I screwed you, I'll tell them you skimmed off the top for yourself. I know the head of your crew – cheat him and he hangs you on a meat hook like Hitler did. Who are they gonna believe? You? A junkie. Or me? I got my friends to stand up for me." He has to know I see through him before he goes any farther down this road.

I let him think it over.

"Look. *Ti capisco.* I have to explain fifty cents. It's less than I told them."

"Tell them you were wrong. It's hot right now. The thing made it hot. You're lucky to get it turned over so fast. I'm getting mine on the back end."

A lie. I couldn't see anything wrong with lying to a junkie. A junkie's whole life is one big lie. I certainly couldn't trust him to go back to his crew and be straight.

I was tired of his game. "I want you to walk out of here."

I summoned Guido, yelling his name.

Guido answered with a shout, "Yeah?"

"Yeah, Guido, come in here for a second."

In came Guido from the storeroom, with his glasses on the tip of his nose and the racing sheet in his hand, wearing his black porkpie hat indoors.

"Guido. I'm giving your friend here a heavy bag. See inside." I opened it for Guido to see the fifty stacks of one hundred $100 bills. "Full of *scarole.* He's leaving now. We wouldn't want anything to happen to all that green once he left, would we?"

Looking at the junkie, Guido replied, *"Sono cavoli tuoi!"* Italian for "it's your neck."

I handed over the bag and took one last look at the junkie. Watery, unfocused eyes. Dry lips. Corners of his mouth sagging. Nose red, with purple veins.

I told him, "Time to go. Our business is finished. Take

this bag and don't come back, ever." He mumbled, "Why you got to be so grumpy?" and ambled out into the afternoon air.

I called out to Guido, who was retreating back into the storeroom, "You got a finder's fee coming your way."

Guido looked over his shoulder and said, "Thanks. I had a rough day at the track."

I once saw a large dog push a small cat up a flight of stairs, the dog using its nose. The dog planted its nose on the cat's rump and kept pushing, though the cat would fall backward after every shove. This continued for several minutes, the dog prodding and pushing, and the cat never gaining any ground. After about three minutes of this, the dog bit the cat's head off and tossed it aside. The cat's headless body fell to the bottom of the stairs. The dog sniffed it and walked away.

In my life, I've often been that dog. No amount of my pushing someone or something else achieves the desired results because a lot of people I've known have been that cat. Yet, I have had to live with those people and situations. There is no way I feel guilty about biting off their heads. That's life. That's the world. Not immoral but amoral. If I choose to succeed or overcome a situation, someone else is going to have to lose. Likely, if I'm not the dog biting off the head, the next person in line dealing with this is going to do it. That was always the end of the story.

I don't regret how I've lived my life, not for a moment. I saw hell on earth – believing in anything except myself was not an option I ever entertained. If I wind up somewhere after I die, in a well of souls, I can't imagine it will be worse than what I've seen already.

A week ago, I was talking to two Jewish guys I know

from business, but both of them raised very proper, Hebrew school and all that. They said the hell for non-Jews was different from their hell. One says Jewish hell is a dark pit, he calls it Sheol. A place where every dead person is cast until the messiah comes – like a holding cell. I know what that's like. Not so bad, not so good. The other Jew interrupts him and says, no, it's not a pit, it's a washing machine! A place he names Gehinnom. There, you get washed up, cleaned from your sins, then go on to heaven. I know how a washing machine works – I could survive a spin and rinse. Either way, no big deal.

Make of that what you will. In the end, the one watching me is me. I save myself. My life is lived with honor, if not totally honorable.

CHAPTER NINETEEN

It's the End

West Thirty-Sixth Street, Manhattan, June 17, 1962

*Most people are about as happy as they
make up their minds to be.*
Abraham Lincoln

He sat in the chair with an awful tiredness, for the moment beyond his ability to get up. Standing was out of the question currently, and he had no thought of walking at this time. He would soon have to empty his bladder. That could wait a little bit more. The chair wasn't comfortable, so it held no seductive attraction to him. It was worn and ratty, like the rest of the room. He would feel the same listlessness, sitting down or standing up. What that chair had going for it was the unsteady wooden table right next to it, on four wobbly, battered legs, not unlike his own legs. The table supported his lone incentive for staying on his rump, and it kept him in that chair.

On the tabletop, crowded together with no empty space between them, were bottles of booze – Scotch, Irish and Canadian whiskey, sweet Kentucky bourbon, a hip flask of Tennessee rye, some cheap California brandy (there was no sane reason for wasting money on a drink that tasted all the same to him now), New York State flavored wine for variety, and a half pint of Jamaican dark rum (in case, because he didn't favor the clear stuff). This was his sustenance for the day, and if he planned it correctly, this would carry him through for another three or four days until his spasm was gone.

The chair, table, and he were in a room in a flophouse on West Thirty-Sixth Street, on the second floor, overlooking the backyard of another flophouse that faced north on Thirty-Seventh. Hell's Kitchen, Dutch Fred the Cop called it while watching a small but bloody street skirmish. Hell is mild, he said, this is Hell's Kitchen, red hot. It stuck: a fit place to flop and be apart from normal human society. Here, the accepted rules of decency lapsed, for a price. People with alley cat behavior were indulged, as commerce.

The room was painted yellow several decades ago, and the floor was covered in the disintegrating fragments of a sheet of brown linoleum that had borne the shoes of hundreds, probably thousands of guests. (How many working girls and their clients had been horizontal in this room? It didn't matter; he wasn't going to be using the bed.) He was a writer, so he referred to his stay here as a sequester, albeit self-imposed.

He drank.

The writer loved his tools of the trade, and he knew most of the words for what he was called: rummy, dipsomaniac, inebriate, boozer, lush, souse, sot, tippler, alcoholic, drunken bum, and on and on. A doctor told him he was suffering from a disease, that his body didn't react to alcohol like other people's did. It was "hypersensitive to the effects of alcohol." The writer told the doctor that was a crock. After all, the writer never suffered an alcoholic haze or a lapse of memory. His mind remained clear and sound, drinking or not and, of course, for most of the time, he wasn't drinking. He knew better: This wasn't an illness. It was a relief. He had what the ancient Greeks called *dipsa*, meaning thirst and a mania for it (therefore, dipsomania). Thus, a natural urge to quench his enduring thirst. It was not a disease, something foreign invading his body – the thirst was there, and every so often it built up to the point where it had to be satisfied. That was natural and innate, the same as eating bread to salve hunger, but the need called less frequently. The spasm came upon him when he finished writing, and it had to be seen to urgently.

This time, a friend invited him to the town of Rye, to dine with a group of writers on Sunday. He suspected this friend was trying to steer him from going into the spasm. And ride the railroad? He begged off, saying, "Why would I travel so far to eat with strangers?"

He had separated himself here to not disturb others or invite prying eyes, and be left alone. His *dipsa* spasm required seclusion to effect treatment. All of his acquaintances, even his best friends and close associates, were aware that the end of a writing assignment meant his disappearance for four or five days.

The record was eight days; however, that time was followed by two weeks in hospital to treat "extreme alcohol poisoning," an experience worse than the dipsomania, which he vowed to never surrender to again for such a prolonged time. He had overdone it. Then there was the time he passed out and burned his arm on a steam pipe, in this very same hotel. That was earned exhaustion, not common drunkenness. He reasoned, five days was enough to chase the *dipsa* spasm away and resume his regular life, without any risks.

No, he was not sick. This was his normal response to his aching thirst, which struck him when his whole being had its fill of the strains of putting the correct words in the right order on pages and pages of whatever he was paid to write. He wasn't an alcoholic. Alcoholics needed booze all the time, with no control. He controlled his thirst until the proper time presented itself for him to take libation. Then he took until the thirst was slacked, and no more. He did admit, to himself, that the one time he didn't control it he paid the price in the hospital, but that was once. He was in control now.

There was a reason, a reasonable explanation for why he drank. The demands of his chosen profession taxed him, physically and mentally, most of all mentally, to produce at a consistently high plateau of achievement. Farmers labored sunup to sundown to get results, and they accepted the rigors of their labors. Workers on an assembly line bore the job requirements that made quality cars and machines; that was what they did and how they lived. Why, bankers banked from nine to three, and a bit after so that finances fueled the system and produced prosperity. Writers were no different. Farmers kept farming hours. Factory workers had unions. Bankers closed their doors at three sharp. Writing was its own special situation, and the writer had special requirements.

Writing professionally was an excruciating, painful, but ultimately rewarding pursuit accompanied by a good measure of sadomasochism that writers admitted to themselves. Selecting each word, because the well-chosen words were heaven, engulfed by the purgatory of the other, flaccid, nagging words crowding them on the page. This was a pitched battle. The agony of rethinking and rewriting hapless words to be suitable for sharing the page with the masterful ones; the expenditure of wit to erase and write again, then blotting some out and trying once again to marshal words to make them say what they must in unison say, to talk back and announce from the page, "This is it!" Often, his characters would speak to him, telling him what to write. That was pleasure and pain. It's the right word that takes the writer to the next word. The words tied together into thoughts, and the thoughts became a story.

Next comes the editor, that self-appointed guardian, juror, and executioner of thought, who always kills partway, taking a centimeter of the writer's skin at a time, leaving the writer bleeding but alive and awake for more of the same. Steinbeck called it "mystical business." Twain termed it "the slavery of pen and paper." More like word-by-word abortion. The writer gives birth, and the editor keeps rearranging the baby's features.

This was "the agony and the sweat" of writing. Is it any wonder the writer drank?

He admitted that not all of his professional compatriots drank, and not all felt what he did. Some did. He knew, and his contemporaries all knew, the story of the most original writer of their generation, a great writer who went to Hollywood to pen screenplays to pay the bills. The great writer was asked by Clark Gable to name the foremost American authors. Among a group of five, the great writer named himself. Gable, caught off guard, asked naively if he was a writer. The great writer replied, "Yes,

Mr. Gable. What do you do?" The great writer grew weary of the hollow movieland grind and was homesick. There came a day when he asked his boss if he could write from home. Not catching the drift, the boss said yes. The great writer packed his bags and went back to Mississippi. He would return west to seek the ink-stained dollar several times.

There were writers who could detach their personal feelings from how and what they wrote. That might work for them, though he considered such an approach cowardly and spineless. He was not so high-minded to believe his own work didn't benefit from a lot of self-editing, and a generous amount of the outsider looking in with a red pencil. That was practical good sense. What he objected to, or rather what he did, was to engage in a match of wills with his editors because, to his way of thinking, no one understood his writing better than the writer himself. The editor was an assistant and had to be reminded of that constantly. The courageous writer had an open mind about suggestions, and a firm grasp of what needed to be on the page. Most of his editors appreciated this tack, if grudgingly. It was a push-pull, a wrangle, sometimes a skirmish, rarely a war. For all that, he never lost an editor, an assignment, or a paycheck.

The aftermath was the *dipsa* spasm. He was drained and needed to replenish his body. It was his shadowy, thirsty season once more.

In his flophouse room, he first received his provisions from the desk clerk – the aforementioned bottles, ordered yesterday. Then he loosened his tie, took off his jacket and shoes, removed his belt, and collapsed. He didn't need cups or ice or food. He was in the company of his treatment. The bottles were old friends, tested, proven loyal, and ever ready to soothe him. Appropriately, it was the day of rest, Sunday. Here was his church, and the bottles were his altar.

The assignment he had that morning completed and mailed was the last installment of a short story series for a national magazine, with a paycheck enough to last for two months before accepting another piece of work. In the story, a man of better than average means, a farm agent in the rural South, is riding a horse named Traveler, one that he has ridden often in the recent past. He and the horse go for a light cantor on the trails around town where both man and horse live. They gallop through fresh greenery and mature trees, shades of green and brown waving as they pass. The man starts thinking to himself about his business and his life and asks why he isn't happier. Traveler begins thinking to itself about why the rider doesn't seem to care where they are going. This prompts the horse to decide they will go where the horse wants to go, to the farm where Traveler was raised, in hopes of catching a glimpse of its mare. The man is so totally absorbed in his own train of thought (*Why can't I be pleased with my success?*) that he ignores the horse. Traveler senses this, and becomes enraged at the rider's thoughtlessness. (*Why can't this human understand that it's a ride if we are in harmony with each other?*) Finally, Traveler, knowing that it is the stronger of the two, starts galloping, gradually forcing the man to take notice. Now the man is panicked – *Where are we? Why are we going so fast? What must I do to take control of what is happening? How is this going to end?* The man pulls on the reins and bends forward to whisper to the horse to slow down.

Traveler understands the man's desire but is too caught up in the frenzy of the gallop, which is now a race to visit its mare. The horse tells itself, *I have feelings too.* It is not in Traveler to cede control back to the thoughtless rider, so Traveler speeds up, and the rider is frightened that his immediate destiny is in the horse's power and not his own. Traveler's nostrils flare. The rider loses his grip on the reins and falls off the horse violently, at an accelerated rate of speed. Fortunately, the rider is wearing a helmet. Unfortunately, he falls forward, under Traveler's hooves.

The rider sees that his hour has come, while Traveler races on to its mare's farm. The rider dies in the middle of the horse trail, not having resolved why he isn't happier. At dusk, a stranger comes upon the man's body, the face showing no injuries and the eyes open, and remarks to no one, "Such a well-dressed rider, you would have thought he knew how not to be outdone by a horse." The errant horse is eventually tracked to the farm, where it is found nuzzling its mare. Traveler rears up at the sight of the captors. Being led back to its stable on the other side of town, Traveler thinks to itself, *It's the end.*

When he wrote that last line, the writer knew his thirst had returned, as it always did at the end of an assignment. He had already booked and paid for the room at the flophouse and put in his order at the liquor store.

Here he sat, a half-empty bottle of Dewar's in his writing hand, gazing at nothing and no one. There was a sharp pain in his stomach that made him think maybe this time he'd end this early. He took another drink and consoled himself: "I'm still in control." Soon he would try to stand up and relieve his full bladder. Soon wasn't easy to calculate. He didn't want to stand. What he wanted to do was go to sleep. His bladder would have to stay full for now. He placed the bottle on the side table and slept in the chair. That was his choice.

His sleep was easy and peaceful, like a free pass out of concern into a new place, a place with which he was unfamiliar. There was no booze and no need to sleep; he was both asleep and fully aware he was sleeping. This he had not felt before. He took this to mean the booze was doing its job effectively because he was so calm and cognizant of his own state. *What a relief*, he thought, *what glorious peace to be so happy*. He wanted to remain like this, hovering above consciousness and sleep, riding both worlds simultaneously. *Bless you, alcohol. Bless you*, he intoned to himself. After a pause, he thought, *But I really do need to get back to the conscious place, that room. Something is waiting for me to do. I have an important job waiting for me.*

Gracefully, without much effort, he pulled himself up from his chair. He blinked and yawned and looked around. The world outside the tattered curtains and the grimy windowpanes was dark and forsaken, akin to an empty pit at midnight in a vast field.

He yawned a second time and looked at his wristwatch. Five hours after he fell asleep? It couldn't be. It was early morning, he remembered. Five hours later should still be light outside.

He pulled away from the chair and went to the bathroom to urinate, first clicking the light switch. He washed his hands and splashed cold water on his face. The face staring back in the mirror needed a shave, desperately. He was confused. Walking into the main room, he found the telephone. He didn't want to speak to anyone; in fact, during a *dipsa* spasm he didn't talk to people, ever. But he had to get clear of a murky fog that swirled in his skull. He had to connect somehow to determine what was what.

He dialed "O" to talk with the front desk.

A disinterested, distracted voice answered with a vacant, "Yeah?"

"What time is it?"

There was an icy silence, indicating the front desk clerk thought he was an idiot for asking. After five silent seconds, the voice replied, "Eight . . . p.m."

His watch must have stopped. *Eight o'clock? At night? What day, what day was it?*

"What day?"

Another icy silence ensued. *You're an idiot and a drunk, leave me alone,* the clerk probably said to himself. The room rate didn't include a delivery boy and a babysitter for a boozehound.

"It's the eighteenth, June 18."

The writer put the receiver back in the telephone cradle hurriedly, banging it in the ear of the clerk, confirming for the recipient again that the writer was liquor addled.

The writer sat down and told himself, *I've been asleep for more than a day.* A pleasant rest of over twenty-four hours that seemed like a nap. Had he awakened too early in the darkness, when everyone else was still asleep? Was he that exhausted? Was it the booze acting on his central nervous system? Over one whole day gone in a wink, well, a series of winks. This hadn't ever occurred previously. Perhaps his capacity for drinking was diminished. Curiously, his next thought was thankfulness for not wetting himself in his sleep. Had he truly been asleep? He couldn't say for sure what had happened. Maybe it was a thing other than sleep, but what? He was still alive.

He thought a couple of minutes while gazing slowly about the room. It was a dump, but an easy place to rest. He was pacified by the familiar threadbare furnishings and the forlornly peeling, faded paint on the ceiling. Was it threadbare and peeling and sad? The words, the right words, were gone. He didn't need them. No one spoke to him except himself. That was what he wanted most, an end to all the nagging words. He realized he was okay to sit quietly. He wasn't thirsty and that was okay as well. He felt a sharp pain in his abdomen. "I'll stay here," he murmured.

He said aloud, "All right," to the walls, floor, and ceiling to reassure himself. *Was it*? he asked himself silently.

There is something important I must do; he recalled thinking that. What was it? The thought had pulled him from his slumber, an important thing to do, waiting for him. This must be something to write about because what else would be so necessary for him to get done, to disrupt so wonderful a sleep? But it didn't come to him. He rolled it around his brain, thinking this and that and the rest – *what was it?*

The fog inside him hung on, like how his thoughts melted into utter confusion while falling asleep. He finished his last assignment, that couldn't be it. He wasn't hungry and he had relieved himself, yet the urgency pressed on him. A task he must do, an imperative feeling in his bones like breathing. This was heavy, weighing him down to the chair. Could it be that pain he felt? It had dissipated, though he still felt the memory of it. No, it had to be more words forcing him to pay attention and look for them. Words burdening him, in pursuit. It was as if all that he had done was now indistinct blurs of light and black. Words stopping him from being in that new place he was in when he slept, the totally gentle place where there was peace, and retreat from all those words that hounded him while awake.

He had to get away again. *The words will have to take care of themselves*, he told himself. There was one solution, and he resolved himself to return.

Sleep overcame him again, one that settled his body thoroughly. The partially empty bottles were his companions. Silently and with respect, they kept a vigil over him as he slipped under. The bottles were celebrants in a requiem. Falling deeply into sleep's arms, his body abruptly sat bolt upright on the chair's edge and toppled onto the unswept floor, causing a pillow of dust to envelop him. Now nothing hurt.

He had vanquished the writer.

This was the rest without end he sought. A voyage through the air to the quiet land he inhabited minutes ago. That place. He wasn't sure he had actually awoken from there to here, but he was going back there, to where he was sure he would be welcomed.

It was Monday. Halfway around the world, an evil wall separated Berlin, symbolizing the fear of humanity being obliterated in an instant. (It was, according to one observer, "unnatural and inhumane.") If the writer had seen it, he would have found the right words to describe it. He didn't. He had no more desire to marshal words and give them life. There was no more to give. Other writers, in other places, set down worried words about us destroying ourselves by the push of a button. He was beyond those cares.

CHAPTER TWENTY

Long Ago

Lily Pond Avenue, Staten Island, May 1, 2019

There's no prize for growing older.
Dr. R. D. Laing

I'm seventy-nine, closer to the end than the beginning.

I don't spend time thinking about going, though I can't seem to help falling asleep at night with the questions of *if* and *where* I will wake up when the sun shines.

Only a damn fool doesn't wonder about death – and I'm no damn fool. Sure, I think about it. I just don't obsess over it. If and when it crosses my mind, it crosses out quickly. I am well aware that in the middle of living we can find ourselves in the waiting arms of death. I read the words of a historian, "We respect death and long to find meaning in it." I do respect it and I'm sure it has meaning, but I've got no time to waste on questions that go in circles. *What's it like, being dead? Well, no one knows; ain't no one ever come back to report – at least no one I know. They're all dead. No one to ask, What's it like, being dead?*

There is this ditty I first heard as a college student

almost sixty years ago: "We shout and scream and wail and cry, but in the end, we all must die." Just so.

I've lived in this place all my life, man and boy. Left for vacations now and then, but always came back here every time. Couldn't find anywhere else to go that ever seemed any better this time around.

Born right here, went to school here, got married and had no kids here, and outlived my spouse here. Here is where I know, and I don't brag that I know much about here. It's a place – a mostly quiet, easy place. I look out my windows at the same scene, maybe sixty years and no great change to shake my view. It's here. I'm here. I do see the bridge, though, for the last fifty-five years. That's quite a sight and the traffic that goes with it. Otherwise, not much new to look at. I'm used to my giant neighbor, the bridge.

The bridge goes to Brooklyn, a place I've gone to a few times, only to come back. Nice place, not that attractive to me. It's too busy. With people I mean. Nothing beats where I live, at the foot of the bridge, for being busy with cars. Cars don't bother me – I don't go out much anymore, so cars aren't an annoyance from my point of view. A whole bunch of people screamed and hollered and got red in the face when the bridge went up, shouting the neighborhood was ruined; before so quiet and removed from the rest of the city, now flooded with traffic. Didn't worry me in the least, not then or after. An island can't survive on its own, cut away from everybody else, and a damned ferry won't suffice. Hooray for the bridge, and that's from a person living most of his life at the foot of one of the world's biggest.

Now, I'm alone for the most part. Oh, hell – all the

time. No wife, never any kids, my relatives either scattered or dead, my friends all announced in the obituaries. The bridge and I are sort of friends, both of us constant memories that life goes on, whether someone else likes it or doesn't. The bridge and me, two seniors in a world of little kids.

Let us get one thing clear: I'm not complaining. Not one bit. I got born alone and I'll likely die alone. That's the way it works, except, of course, for twins who automatically have a partner to start with, but even so, eventually, they're alone in life too. And in death. But I don't complain about loneliness. Loneliness is different from being alone. Loneliness is a state of mind. Alone is a physical condition. If it's just a picture of my late wife, I have company. I have memories to keep me company: powerful, breathing memories. Memories occupy most of my time. They're good memories too. They keep me warm and secure.

Other people are plagued by their memories. There's a woman down the hall from me. She's eighty-two, but still spry and with her faculties, I think. Now and then, she tells me she sees a man with a knife lurking at her door. I've never seen him; she swears she has. Could be that she's the one who wants to see him. Could be he's a bad memory that she can't shake in her loneliness. I don't judge. Whether or not what she says she sees is flesh and blood, she does see it, I am convinced of that. She's scared, not crazy. Even if I can't see it doesn't mean it doesn't exist. I have no right to proclaim myself sane and call her mad. I pray for her.

I'm talking about loneliness and death, but I don't mean to dwell on it. It ain't that important, compared to, say, eating. Yeah, eating. Think about it. We eat every day (well, almost all of us) and more than once a day. I'll throw in drinking and it's practically nonstop from morning to bedtime. Eating. Certainly, a happier topic than loneliness and death. Let us call death the end of eating, because I can't say what we eat in the next place, heaven or that other joint, or if we eat.

To me, eating is a gift from our creation, to which we carelessly give little proper attention. Do you stop to taste each bit of food and drink, including sweet, cool, refreshing water, you put in your mouth? Is your fork a shovel or a delicate instrument? Do you honor what you consume by pausing to look at it, smell its aroma, and let it roll around your tongue to get all the flavors? I wager not.

The act of dining (or, I should say, the fine art of dining) is amazingly complicated; its joys are many and profound. Who you dine with. Where it happens. Why and how. Unfold the layers of a meal, discover the depths of your life, your precious daily life. It's living every day, living awake, that prompts the poet to write, "I ate, drank and was merry while death kept the till." I've run up my tab, enjoying it all as best I could.

I like to remind myself that the Lord Christ, in His full knowledge and will, invited His own betrayer to dine with Him at the Last Supper. He could have said, "Judas, you're going to turn me in anyway, so why don't you skip this one. I'd like to dine in peace with my real friends." Of course, the other eleven men at the table would all abandon Him immediately after His arrest, except Peter, who would deny knowing Him three times before His execution. Not such a pleasant meal! He loved the world enough to share a meal with Judas. I'd have to overcome an enormous anger in me to do that. I don't think I have the strength to be that gentle.

But – this was a supper that would be repeated billions, if not trillions of times over the following two thousand years. The bread and blood of life, of remembrance. In its way, it continues to combine eating and immortality in a union that feeds lots of souls. The Lord's table is the original soul food!

Just what is soul food? What does it mean? The famous queen of soul food, Sylvia Woods, of Harlem's Sylvia's Restaurant, was asked what made soul food, soul food. She replied, "It's prepared with love!"

The soul is filled with love. There is love in food. It's fulfilling love; the memories of it expel loneliness.

Love isn't sold by the pound or used by the pinch. I do know I can tell when love is added; not necessarily by how it makes food taste, but by how it makes me feel.

My mother and grandmother cooked with love – there are dishes they made that remain instant reminders to me of their hearts and souls. How my grandmother could fry a freshly killed chicken on a Sunday for dinner after Mass, or make deviled eggs (what a paradox!) for church suppers. Certainly, my grandmother used flour and salt and pepper, and piping hot shortening like other cooks. Her eggs were deviled with mustard and mayonnaise and topped with paprika. My mother baked loaves of white bread that, right out of the oven and slathered with sweet butter, were more pleasing than store-bought cake. Her bread, much the same as other cooks' bread, was composed of flour, yeast, eggs, salt, butter, and a touch of sugar. Nothing remarkable in any of these ingredients. This food is memorable enough to remain on my taste buds and survive to this day. I'm never alone with these memories.

My beloved aunt, who was Jewish, roasted chicken; the memory of its taste prompts me, in my imagination, to slap other chicken roasters everywhere. She showed me how she plumped the raw chicken, pouring boiling water over and in it, from a teakettle, by a technique, she assured me, she learned from her mother, and so on back into her family's generations of cooks. She never burned her hands, though she plumped without gloves over the sink. She practiced magic! Whatever spices she used besides salt and pepper remain unknown, but the end result was the juiciest, sweetest roast chicken, with the crispiest skin because of the plumping, I ever ate in my life.

The other day, I looked through scripture and surprised myself with the miraculous significance of eating in the Gospels. Apart from the Last Supper, Christ turned water into wine for His first recorded miracle. He fed the crowd with the loaves and fishes; John's gospel may well have been written forty to sixty years after that event, perhaps in the lifetimes of a number who witnessed it. Upon His resurrection, He made breakfast for the disciples on the shore. On that occasion, He forgave Peter and made him the leader of the first church.

That's how I spend my time nowadays. Thinking and remembering, musing on my life throughout the years. With my Social Security, I have just enough money to care for myself, and I'm rich – the memories are my investments, now paying dividends.

Like I said, I don't cross the bridge often. Last month, with a companion's help, I ventured to Flushing Meadows Park in Queens, the site of the 1965 World's Fair. I remember going there in my twenties, with my parents, as a treat for them. They had attended the first New York World's Fair there in 1939. My memories of the 1965 version are centered around the joy of eating – Bel-Gem waffles with whipped cream and strawberries; the Chun King Inn, with salty fried rice for ninety-nine cents as lunch; the Brass Rail hotdog stands, topped by giant balloons, that were very different from greasy city push-carts; free samples of sparkling Fresca grapefruit soda; and the Top of the Fair, the most elegant place there. I also saw my first Ford Mustang, and how I desperately wanted to drive one. I enjoyed watching how thoroughly delighted my parents were, more than I enjoyed it by myself. They giggled and grinned like teenagers. I came back three times, though none of those visits was as happy as this first one.

For a Catholic family like us, the highlight of the fair was the Vatican pavilion. The pope himself, John XXIII, gave permission for Michelangelo's sculpture of Mother Mary holding Jesus, the *Pietà*, to be transported to be shown. Paul VI visited the installation in 1965 to bless it. My parents and I stood in awe of this incredible devotional artwork; we were at peace in a space perfectly silent and reverent. It seemed all of us held our breath in its sight. What a touching memory I have of my parents at that moment.

Returning to the park now, the images poured over me. I tasted the foods again. I saw my parents holding hands as we strolled the fair's wide boulevards. I was back in time. At the former location of the Vatican pavilion stood a circular granite bench, inscribed to the two popes who had made the pavilion possible, mounted by three large curved stone steps. The bench was called an exedra, the name in Greek for a place of meditation. My friend and I were the only people there, joined by the occasional pigeon.

I sat. The memories were alive. I heard the voices, not just my parents' but all the fairgoers, their excited, thrilled voices talking and laughing over and around each other, on a brilliant day in a vast open space; what almost thirty years before had been a pile of ashes and garbage was then a sparkling and green new site. The fair remained, in the fullness of an experience, as alive, real, and intimate for me now as half a century ago.

I thought to meditate. Meditation. I knew how to pray – prayer was praising and asking, so meditation was waiting. I could wait; that's what I do naturally. Waiting for what, I did not know, but waiting all the same. My time had not come to go, and I wasn't contemplating that anyhow. It was a beautiful day, far too satisfying to wait for going. I sat and thought of nothing for quite some time. The sunshine played on my face and made my cheeks and the backs of my hands browner.

My friend drove me back home. The attendants and aides asked me about my trip. Perhaps they were genuinely interested. I related my impressions of that place, but not my inner thoughts and emotions. I had spent time with my parents, and that was personal, not sentimental. Sentiment is what is lost, but longed for emptily. Memory is what you have and choose to keep vibrant and close.

My mind became filled with anticipation of what was for dinner. Set before me was fish and bread. Simply grilled whole fish and oven-warm bread, crusty and chewy, bread with character and bite. Nourishing bread and moist fish, a meal from a distant past. I last had it in the presence of others, in a furnished upper room in a stone house on the western hill. Or was it next to the olive grove in the garden? Before the meal, my feet were washed. I dipped my bread in oil. I ate my fish with my hands. I drank wine poured by the Host.

I was the thirteenth guest, the fourteenth person in the cenacle. If you want to know what I know, we were all betrayers. Yet, I was invited to partake.

These were gradual memories, taking me, in measured steps in the end, to a life I once lived and savored.

CHAPTER TWENTY-ONE

Treasures

American Museum of Natural History, Manhattan, Fall 1989

Someone else will . . .
lead you where you do not want to go.
John 21:18

You pile up what you value in life and then it comes tumbling down, turning into worthless dust.

Perhaps you value your job, your house, your bank account, your smarts, or, if you're young, your family. Your precious, caring parents and your siblings. Your perfect family – they are your pride in the world and the expression of your life. All of your heart is filled with your family.

And then, it falls away.

My family was my treasure at eighteen; every inch of my soul was woven into my wonderful mother and father, and my older brother. They were wise and gentle, the answer and refuge in my young life. They were my all in all. I was proud of them, but not only of them, but also to be sheltered and raised by them. My family was all I needed and everything I wanted.

And then, they fell away.

When I was eighteen, deliberately then because I had reached the age of consent and college, my parents divorced, exposing in a moment's time the collapsed foundations of my love and pride. My mother was a closet alcoholic. She drank to excess in secret, after hours and behind closed doors. Her constant drowning in booze was expertly kept hush-hush. In response, my father who did know, was a stray cat, implanting himself regularly in the wives of family friends and my mom's female buddies. This, I learned to my utterly explosive surprise, and disappointment and disgust, had been going on for years. The parental kisses at holiday parties. The dinners for the four of us in our home. The vacation trips to the Catskills. Christmas gatherings. Shopping trips in the station wagon. All frauds. A hidden dense web of frauds, spun by my deceptive parents, done they said, for our own good. I was too in love with them to see them as they really were. They unmasked themselves before my innocent eyes. To misquote the baseball genius Billy Martin, "One lies and the other one swears to it."

My world was emptied in the time between my laughter and my tears.

An aching crater in my heart sucked out my soul, like an imploding star. This vast hole of emptiness took what had been the massive, solid structure of my life and replaced it with a vacuum of dead space. Not a space filled with scraps or ruins, not with burned timbers and ashes – just vacant space. Null and void.

This vacancy within me, this hole in my soul, was a place unoccupied by anything, other than my anguish. Terminal self-pity was my new tenant. The tenant that paid no rent and, instead, took from me like a squatter from an unwilling land owner. I got no compensation for the residency and the illegal occupant set about destroying the premises and bankrupting the host, with careless ferocity.

My family came apart with frightening speed and thoroughness, and vanished as if it never truly existed. What was gone wasn't only their presence – the memories disappeared as well. My family never had been what for eighteen years I believed with my heart it was. Now, it wasn't ever.

My home and my spirit were vaporized, like so many smashed atoms after a nuclear blast. I had no lifeline, no anchor, no ladder and no rope. I died emotionally, yet once my soul was gone, it continued to die over and over again every waking minute. Like the tragic myth of Prometheus, my soul was pecked out every day, to regrow and be pecked out endlessly forever.

I attended college because my parents, during the time when they had acted like parents, set aside funds and plans, with encouragement and moral support, to ensure I would be educated appropriately. They weren't rich, nor had they ever acted like they were, but their solid middle-classness imposed on me the understanding that a college education was required in our family. That, of course, was when I absolutely knew their love was eternal and their caring word was law. With that gone, I was still required to submit and obey their broken mandate for me, absent the family that once was and now was not to be – there wasn't another choice for a dependent teenager.

The college experience was actually a type of balm for my lost soul – at school, I was surrounded by half-teens/half- soon adults, who, I discovered, were almost all nursing shattered hearts and dry souls; bottomless beings, lost and not found.

I also discovered booze and sex. Both were available and abundant: my fellow students possessed prodigious appetites for those commodities, much as we craved and sought milk and bread in our earlier lives. The now necessary vices were in ready supply at school.

My college days weren't spent in a drug induced daily haze, though. I knew my limits in the bars and in bed. I would not be self-destructive. If at all, I wanted to live for the purpose of constant self-numbing, and my fear of death. Perhaps I would kill myself slowly, reaching a no return from total loss of the will to live, in the future; swift determined death, however, wasn't my bag. The misery was in itself a reward for my hollowness. I earned my misery and I was ready to wallow in it, for as long as I wanted.

I ceased to communicate with my parents. I suppose their squalid shame made them accept my silence. They deserved this. They knew what they had perpetrated. My brother was four years ahead of me leaving home and graduating from college. He made his own life and, I speculate, knew what mom and dad were about well before the coming out party. If so, the bastard didn't tip me to the truth. Thus, he and I separated and didn't speak.

I replaced my memories of a family pretense with an alternate pretense that my family never existed. I think my brother did the same, only sooner than me. He and I were likely two minds with the same notion: those memories were a sham. To hell with them. Rather than live with the humiliation of what once was, we both dismissed this parent scam and regarded that life as something that hadn't happened.

One side effect was I could not trust anyone, not even myself, with my vulnerabilities. Having female company was a mile wide and a millimeter thick – lots of women could be fun and physically enjoyable. They could not come too close emotionally, nor dwell too deeply in me. They could be friendly, but not friends. Sexy, but not loving, and allowed to be around me, but not to be with me. For the most part, this meant shallow relations and not relationships. I built a concrete encasement for my evacuated soul, thick enough to keep me, as well as everyone else, out.

The end of college, a not so spectacular event that nonetheless resulted in a soulless, moderately educated functioning adult, found me living in Manhattan's Yorkville, on my own and materially sufficient and comfortable. My apartment was above the Elk Candy Company, an antiquated glass storefront shop, with a popular window display of edible marzipan creations of fruits, flora and fauna for the ogling of passersby on East 86th Street. In the evenings, the zither players, German-American bands and noisy revelers blared exuberantly out of the restaurants, dance halls and bars, giving a throbbing beat to the teeming, streetlamp lit sidewalks. I came to reside here by chance (and affordability) and stayed because it fed me great food, provided loads of strangers with whom I could get lost in a crowd, and featured a reliable supply of quality watering holes with willing women.

My recreation, other than nightly bar hopping, was extended neighborhood walks, mostly on weekends. To the east was Carl Schurz Park and the East River, that wasn't a river but an estuary between the Long Island Sound and New York Bay. There were benches facing the water where I sat and people-watched often in warm weather. Walking west, I stopped along Park Avenue to look into stores whose merchandise I couldn't afford. I'd stroll slowly to Central Park and enter the Metropolitan Museum, where there was usually an exhibit or two to hold my attention. I might skip the Met and go on, meandering through the park, touching base with the joggers around the reservoir or pausing to soak in the sun on the Great Lawn. Many days found me on the west side of the park, going to the American Museum of Natural History, stopping to admire Teddy Roosevelt on horseback at the entrance. TR appeared ready for battle, rain or shine.

The Natural History Museum became my favorite attraction. Unlike the elegant, sprawling and somewhat formal confines of the Met, I found the Natural History Museum cavernous and inviting – vast inside and filled with fascination; intimate enough to develop a sense of where things were and what they introduced to me. Being inside was being in the midst of a giant, old-fashioned collection of collections, assembled, it seemed, by an eccentric who looted various places and cultures to show to friends. It was homey and dusty. I appreciated that it didn't boast wealth, which the Met surely did, but it boasted knowledge and grit, much the same as TR. The museum became my private graduate program. I took in whole sections at a time, returning on successive days to steadily absorb the exhibits' lessons, coordinating in my mind the intricate details to form a scope of what I was learning. It was there, not at college, that my love of education was kindled.

It was there that I first saw a totem pole, in the Northwest Coast Hall. It reached to the ceiling, commanding me to look up, up and squint at the carved figures at the top. I was filled with awe, seeing this object that I read about as a little boy, in drawings, descriptions and tales of faraway natives – a staggering hunk of someone's life, a red cedar trunk decorated and painted, fearsome in its size, though simultaneously human and appealing, a gift from the past to the present. I was struck dumb. I owned no words to understand it. It reached out to me, as I cowered in wonder. I came back to it a dozen times in two weeks to stare, because it drew me to be with it. It was imposing and humbling. And mesmerizing.

I began to study its meaning, using the museum's guidebooks. The word totem meant kinship groups. It was a statement in a visual language, full of messages and symbols – the preservation of a complicated cultural story in a statue, rather than in a book. The totem broadcast to the present and future important parts of a personal history, like a telegram from revered elders, over multiple generations, carved in wood to withstand time. It spoke of family and life, carrying a story of hope that descendants would live to hear – these memories were an inheritance of God's grace in their ancestors' lives.

In the museum's library I researched the symbols on my first totem (dating from the 1880s), from bottom to top:
- Whale
- Bullhead
- Ancient powerful supernatural being

- Frog
- Raven
- Salmon
- Seal
- Two-headed serpent
- Frog
- Bear spitting up wolf man
- Killer whale
- Thunder bird man.

There were dozens of totems in the museum, each possessing a unique set of messages about families and occurrences. Cumulatively, they informed me that they weren't silent and they weren't dead. They told me their lives and I, regretfully, didn't want to admit to mine.

Gradually, I found the intricate meanings. The animals were guides for the natives. The animals' physical attributes represented the connections between natives and nature: different animals manifested their qualities in humans as these skills were needed to face life's challenges. Salmon, for instance, might mean a significant catch of fish that saved the natives from starvation. Bear spitting up wolf man may have been a native's escape from ursine clutches, with the swift cunning of a wolf. To the natives, the animals and their guidance were blessings.

The totems stayed with me. The deeper I dug into their stories, the more anguish I felt in my own. I hadn't left me – the concrete tomb inside me began to crack. Whether I loved or treasured it or not, I had a history. I had treasures in me. Tarnished and bent, some of them grotesque and wanton, my treasures remained.

Study of the totems led me to the story of the

Northwest Coast native practice of the potlatch. This ceremony of excessive displays of wealth and giving signified a native life transitional event – a birth, a legal matter, recovery from a disaster, the suffering of a loss, a marriage, a bountiful harvest. The potlatch was performed to demonstrate the giver's power and position of esteem, to show face and cover defeat, to celebrate the miraculous. Enormous amounts of goods, food, music, dancing, and oratory were either given to another group, often natives who had helped the giver in crisis, or the material items were burned in public in a display of destruction of wealth. For several generations, this ceremony was banned by the Canadian government because of its seeming wastefulness. But it was restored in the 1950s, though it had continued sub rosa before then. Potlatch, like totems, was an essential, life affirming element of that native existence, a key to the past and a voice in the here and now. Doing away with material treasure became spiritual strength. The natives unburdened themselves of things to come back into grace.

The totems became part of my daily life. They taught me family was my essence. I couldn't erase what was encoded in me. Treasure the best parts, try to understand the troubling bits, make peace within myself. Grow and endure. Move forward with what I discern. The totems were my teachers. They were wise elders who were proud not to forget the good and the bad. They survived and they thanked God. They saw into me and knew what I was. I couldn't hide from them. Their example filled the gap left by my parents' absence and my anger. They made me see my chosen condition; I was forced to look at myself, as I had looked at the totems at first. They were still alive in old age and I was willfully dead in my meager youth. I was a pitiful malingerer, not a strong survivor. In what did I believe?

I was overwhelmed. I came to this place and knowledge, I was drawn to it, not understanding what my will really was. My genetic building blocks were talking to me. The totems spoke. Eventually, I listened respectfully. The lessons of the totems survived and so should I.

In the late fall of 1989, I sat among these totems and opened my conscience for examination. I was convicted: my crime of injustice against my family was matched by my injustice against myself. By disdaining who I was, I injured my own soul. I rummaged through my file box of college records and found a partially torn Polaroid of my family, a picture I initially ripped and intended to trash, but didn't. I had my brother's last address and hoped he still lived there. I mailed it to him and cried through that night.

CHAPTER TWENTY-TWO

Henry Chu and the Mayor: A Grim Tale

Chinatown, Manhattan, July 5, 2017

*Most of the evil in this world is done by people
with good intentions.*
T. S. Eliot

Mayor Warren Wilton Jr. was shaking outstretched hands excitedly, wading into the midst of citizens, meaning voters, in the afternoon shadow of the Manhattan Bridge in the Lower East Side neighborhood of Chinatown. A century ago, this was Little Italy and home to many newly arrived Jewish residents. Now it was absorbed into the ever-expanding Chinatown that once was on its border and now defied all borders. Little Italy or Chinatown, the streets didn't change – narrow, crooked, broken down, and dirty. The accents and smells were different.

Chinatown on the Lower East Side was the destination of immigrants – legal, illegal, and unknown – from the province of Canton in China, in contrast to the Chinatowns in northeast Queens and Brooklyn's southwest side, which attracted the influx from Fujian Province. The yin and yang of these principal destinations and sources of new

Chinese-Americans, with and without papers, could be difficult to discern for observers lacking an awareness of the cultures.

(The heroic Jewish people who once filled these streets were set free by their parents, never to see them again, to come to America. The Chinese now living here came as a unit, parents and children, but cut off from centuries of expressions of their rich, proud culture. Sing praises in honor of the bravery of both sets of survivors.)

Nowadays, many Cantonese in New York City are second, third, and fourth generation: children college-educated and earning substantial salaries, mother and father clinging to the anchor of their Manhattan apartment to stay in contact with their culture: the food, the temples, the organizations. Incomers to Queens and Brooklyn from Fujian were much more recent arrivals: kids in elementary, middle, and high schools with parents each working manual labor jobs, often away from home during the workweek. The children were usually raised Monday through Friday by paid "aunts" and "grandmas." Manhattan Chinatown's expansion did, however, include many from Fujian.

The political center of New York's Chinese-Americans was Manhattan. The generations built political and social networks with inroads to the two major parties, helping elect mostly Democrat candidates locally and tapping into government money and access to the bureaucracy's social service programs.

That was why New York City's Mayor Wilton was glad-handing on the streets this sweltering July day, looking for the voters. It was one year since his reelection, but it was always the right day to show the mayoral flag and touch flesh with the voting public. Elected politicians, first and foremost, need to be reelected or elected to the next higher office. The mayor was no different. Moreover, he was in need of a little voter love since his public declaration that the city's elite specialized high schools weren't "colorful" enough, and maybe the rigorous entrance exams were somehow biased against blacks and browns. Asians weren't his color of choice. They didn't self-identify as victims.

A wobbly screw in that declaration was the undeniable fact that while blacks and browns neither took those entrance exams nor passed them in proportion to their numerical presence in the city's population, Asian-American kids, and especially Chinese-American kids, sat for the same exams in numbers far greater than their segment of the citizenry. They also passed the exams with flying colors in numbers multiple to their population rank. They made up 59 percent of entrants who passed the test. In fact, as a statistical "minority," Asian-American kids were public education aces.

There was a reason. Their parents sweated bullets at work, hard work, to pay for books and computers and tutors to support academic success. In their two-room Chinatown apartments, side by side with their home shrines, could be found shelves stacked with trophies for chess club participation, math Olympiads, dean's lists, perfect attendance, and honor rolls. Home late from work, exhausted parents gazed at these symbols of their offspring's educational achievements as if the cheap plated-gold figurines were really solid fourteen karat. If anyone wanted to know why so many Asian-American kids earned entry to the city's elite high schools, one need only see the parents earning, striving, saving, and investing. They browbeat and uplifted their children. Substantial numbers of these parents were classified as poor by government-reported standards. The designation of poor did not tell the whole story.

These parents were living, breathing, working proof that willing people can find gainful employment, wake up on time every day, and stay with it, even if they couldn't speak English. They can save and budget. They can succeed as parents, though not wealthy, to raise law-abiding, intelligent, and prosperous children. Immediate lack of money did not mean failure or hopelessness for the future. There was always work for those who would do it. Being poor is a debilitating state of mind called victimhood – victims favored complaining over doing, supposing someone would have to appear and pick them up. Others understood that restaurant dishes needed washing. Clothes needed mending and pressing. Fruits and vegetables had to be sold. Wages must be used wisely. Excitements, fleeting pleasures, and luxuries had to be postponed or denied. New sneakers and the latest cellphones never took precedence over math books and tuition. The future, their children's future, was the first priority.

In China, there is a saying, "America is rich soil. If you are willing to plow it, there is never a lack of land."

For reasons that baffled the Chinese immigrants, many American-born kids and their parents didn't see life this way. For the newcomers and their families, the dream of success was alive and thriving. There was no excuse for chain poverty. Those who wanted to made it out. They did and the government was no help, except for keeping the general peace, most of the time.

This brings us to Henry Chu. He was not a victim.

Henry was thirteen, in his final year in middle school on the Lower East Side. He was the son of Mei Wong Chu and her husband, Gary Chu, second-generation Chinese-Americans from Guangzhou, with citizenship, living on Doyers Street in Chinatown above the noodle shop where Gary was a cook and Mei Wong a waitress. In their estimation, life was pretty good. Yes, they both worked ten to twelve hours a day for six days, and they were grateful to do it. The noodle shop boss owned the building and rented them the apartment.

(In contrast, the mayor and his family lived in the police-protected, walled confines of Gracie Mansion and owned residential property in Brooklyn worth over a million dollars. While he raged publicly about the city's rapacious landlords, he charged his tenants rents at the very top of the hot market for a trendy neighborhood. Despite his unalloyed affluence, the mayor and his family played the victim card as often as they pleased.)

Henry was the Chus' one son, a prize from the gods. A boy, to continue his father's name and bloodline. His Cantonese family, and ancestors watching from above, could not have been happier. He was dutiful and studious, a hard worker at school with a spotless attendance record. His parents' every ambition for him was being fulfilled; their every sacrifice and struggle for him was being rewarded.

Henry's face was framed by big ears that stuck out on the sides like the open doors on a taxicab. He wore glasses that slid down his broad, flat nose, the same as tens of millions of southern Chinese. His thin lips guarded perfect white teeth, the first in his whole family, courtesy of

American dental care. He was not muscular, science and chess being his favorite extracurricular sports. He could play basketball, but not very well. He liked it all the same.

He was bound for the Bronx High School of Science.

Bound that is until Mayor Wilton's declaration. Despite being 12 percent of the city's population, of whom approximately 26.6 percent were poor (the highest poverty rate of all city ethnicities), more than 60 percent of students who passed the test and were to be admitted to the Bronx Science freshman class were of Asian descent. The results were published and Henry's parents went to the Buddhist temple on Mott Street to give an offering of rejoicing.

Being observant Buddhists, they accepted the difficult lesson of the Heart Sutra:

> All things are empty;
> they are neither born nor die,
> neither pure nor impure,
> neither increasing nor decreasing.

The wheel of life had turned in their family's favor. They were thankful.

(The mayor and his wife, Chanika, who resembled a version of the Wicked Witch of the West sculpted by Hershey's, worshipped at a different altar. Their faith was in the revolution; their testaments, social justice, and organizing the masses. They pilgrimaged to Marxist San- dinista Nicaragua so that they could vigorously consum- mate their passionate union under grim portraits of Lenin and Daniel Ortega and pledge their commitment with their upraised fists over the Book of Marx. That was decades ago, but the fire of their communist zeal still blazed

brightly. The mayor still quoted Karl Marx in public.)

Something happened now in New York City, between the announcement of the test results and the September entrance date, to turn the Chu family's wheel of life once more.

Henry's score of 98.75 percent was thirty-fifth on the list of the entrants. The mayor's new plan for the city's specialized high schools now decreed that in the interest of equality and diversity, a quota of these top-scoring students would be limited so that a cohort of "deserving minority students, who were not expert 'test-takers,' could fill these slots." After all, the mayor reasoned, "minority students were not adequately represented in specialized high schools because of a pattern of institutionalized racism in admission practices and a biased entrance examination." Math, you see, was racist. He ordered his education chancellor to proclaim that students of Chinese ancestry succeeded in public schools because they were "imitating" white people – an assertion based on no grounds other than coffee grounds. *(Neither the chancellor nor the mayor nor their allies considered that a racist statement or an expression of institutionalized Marxism, pitting ethnic groups against each other to foster class warfare.)* The chancellor himself was an avowed Marxist, with a Spanish-speaking background. Once again, the mayor had a unique definition of the word "minority," one that didn't include persons of Asian descent. Henry, and those like him, weren't important to the mayor's narrative of who should be protected by government. Who needed their votes?

The mayor found willing believers in the state legislature who ratified this rationale and converted it into new law. The Democrat majority leaders of the state senate and assembly, two closet-socialist African-Americans, fell over each other to pander to the hard-core, dependent, left-leaning Democrat voters in the city, not to mention the benefits of the enormous slop bucket of campaign cash and Election Day assistance provided by labor unions and social welfare lobbyists. From this, the legislators fed at the trough and wallowed in their own excrement. Strangely, these same legislators could not smell their own high-to-heaven stink, but they were hypersensitive to the foul odors they perceived on others who dared to not submit to the government's direction for the masses. The citizens worked for the government, not the other way around – when would the unwashed horde, who weren't feeding on the fetid scraps from the big government buffet, wise up? Indeed, the most harmful people are usually the ones who announce, "I'm harmless." The leader of the New York state senate declared at a public gathering, "I am yours. I am your instrument." In 1938, Hitler said exactly the same thing at a rally.

Henry found himself diverted to his third choice for specialized high school, Brooklyn Tech in Fort Greene, a four-year destination closer geographically to his home than the Bronx. "We're doing you and him a favor by locating him nearer to his home with a shorter daily commute," the Department of Education bureaucrats informed his dejected parents.

(Mayor Wilton's son several years before passed the specialized schools entrance test and attended Brooklyn Tech. At that time, New York City Public Advocate Wilton voiced no criticism of the test's fairness. Throughout his political life, he decided to ignore the truth that all his ideas

for good in the world came with price tags, for which others paid. Not only with the costs, but also the consequences.)

So, Henry and his parents were disheartened and Mayor Wilton was elated. The masses loved him – at least those city dwellers he believed composed the masses.

But it really wasn't the masses who worshipped him. It was his perception of who the masses were. His latest reelection landslide was 66.5 percent of the 23.9 percent of eligible voters who turned out at the voting booth, a major majority of a minor minority. In fact, he was reelected by a staggeringly tiny 16 percent of registered voters. The vast, silent, and major percentage of voters didn't bother to show up – the outcome was foreordained, and they knew it. New York City would elect a Democrat, absent a third-party endorsement and a second line on the ballot to upset the status quo. In the seventy-two years since La Guardia, the city had elected three Republican mayors: each one had been lifted to victory by running on a second ballot line. Wilton was the Democrat now, and a self-identified rabid socialist.

He shook hands, often those of confused citizens caught up in his stage-managed public appearance, many of whom didn't speak English. This meant nothing to a mayor with a self-proclaimed mandate to rule, the luxury of union donations, the backing of the city's most radical segment, and an agenda for government to correct all of society's mistakes and inequalities. He was an apostle honored in his own country.

Henry Chu happened to be in the middle of the mayor's appearance in the neighborhood. Henry hadn't meant to be in this position. He was trying to get to the playground across the street from the federal courthouse to play basketball. School was out for summer, and he adjourned his daily online chess lesson to be with his friends outside in the sun. Now having upset Henry's life once, the mayor was frustrating him again.

The neighborhood kids were drawn to the commotion the mayor's presence was causing. They too were attempting to get close to him and shake his hand.

Ask any police officer or Secret Service agent about the recklessness of a politician in a crowd and you will hear the stories of the elected *(who believe they are anointed)* moving ahead of their protection, the energy of the voters' responses propelling politicians without fear to wade into the adoring crowds. They repeated to themselves, *They love me. I know they love me!*

Henry was squeezing through the knot of citizens, with his friend who lived down the block. Night and day, summer and winter, rain and shine, his friend always wore his blue Yankees jacket, and he had it on today. It was two sizes too big on him because he inherited it from his deceased older brother. He and Henry pushed through to where Mayor Wilton was smiling and politicking. A metal object was jostled out of the friend's jacket pocket and fell to the ground.

As if by instinct or maybe fate, Henry bent down quickly, recovered the fallen object, and tried to give it back to his friend. Henry didn't stop to recognize what the object was. He only knew it fell from his friend's jacket.

Passing from Henry's hand to the other boy, the object fired and fell to the ground a second time, firing again.

The forces of the universe, the spirits of those passed, and infinite justice directed the bullets from the object into the mayor's abdomen and groin. In milliseconds the mayor's public grin became a gruesome sneer, the pain of the shots traveling up his spine and flooding his brain.

In agony, Mayor Wilton cried out, "Not me! No, not me!" as he slumped to the asphalt. *(The mayor detested guns, excepting, of course, the numerous guns that guarded him and his family twenty-four hours a day. There were many who did want to kill him, but their love of liberty replaced their taste for just retribution.)*

A swarm of New York City police officers encircled Wilton. One astute officer began searching with his eyes those present and the surroundings to locate the weapon. It was there, on the ground amid a tangle of legs and feet, attached to no one, attributable to no individual. It was an orphan, homeless, sad, and vulnerable. Even though the officer knew a gun never killed anyone, he couldn't single out the shooter, especially when, in a brief moment, everyone who could took flight away from the scene. A hundred dedicated officers could not have stopped the stampede, leaving the mayor, beloved of a sliver of the electorate, to bleed to death in a circle of members of his police force, a force he once warned his own son to beware of, as a victim. There were twelve cops to witness the mayor meeting his expiration date.

Where now were his voters and their faith in him? The evangelism would have to go on without his leadership. What a pass – to not be a proletarian martyr. He died at the hands of anonymous.

How now would his gospels of income equality, racial awareness, and community activism be preached to a starving city? The messiah was passing, but this one wasn't coming back. In this unique way, the mayor was finally a victim.

In his last grasps at life, Mayor Wilton thought, *I made plans*. He brought his hands up to his face and intoned, "Useless. All useless." Traveling to the next reality, he wished to meet his heroes – Marx, Castro, Mao – on the other side and he did, but not where he thought.

(If he had lived, Mayor Wilton would have delivered his state of the city address the following February, in the hall of the American Museum of Natural History. He would have blamed everyone except himself for his governing failures, homelessness, rising crime, explosion of gun murders, assaults galore, increased public fear, lack of affordable housing, and the rest. Canny observers would have noted the symbolism of a giant dead whale suspended over him when he spoke.)

Henry ran home. His parents were still at work. He turned on the streaming news and watched replays of the events he had been a part of in real time. A crowd of people around the mayor. Two shots. A force of blue-clad police hovering over the body. A mass exodus of the citizenry. Over and over this played on the screen, until it became a video game – *Shoot the Mayor and Run*.

The late mayor's wife, upon viewing the shell in the street that once was her husband the mayor, remarked to no one in particular, "Get that out of here. It's my turn now." *(Her unique accomplishment in city government, other than sleeping with the mayor, was her squandering of $900 million of taxpayer money in one year on an initiative that produced no documented record of results, no recipients, no controls, and no accounting or audit trail. The sheer volume and velocity of her artful trick astonished many of her victims and impressed her party allies; that* *and the fact she faced no consequences, save her husband's public congratulations for her efforts. She was an adept magician, capable, with a brief nod and a twitch of her upturned nose, of making mountains of other people's money vanish without a trace. She invariably mistook her own avarice for power as altruism for the needy, because she was firm in her belief that others must do what she said to do, not what she did. She and her husband were talented manipulators, using fear and greed to bend the voters and collar them.)* She ran to fill his term and was successful with an even smaller percentage of the electorate than her dead husband predecessor. "I'll show them," she promised in victory. Her husband's death, though certainly regrettable to some, was a minor sideshow in the revolution.

Mayor Wilton was grieved and laid to rest. The Police Department was roundly criticized and excoriated in the media, but in time the mystery lost the public attention and the guilty remained unidentified. The police generally got the blame for everything bad that happened in the city. In the opinion of an extreme but loud few, they should be replaced by social workers! *(One can imagine a social worker facing a fentanyl addict holding a gun to a pregnant woman's belly, with the social worker asking, "What are your feelings?" and the woman replying, "My feelings or his?")* New York City stumbled on as it always did, like a drunk on the precipitous ledge of a subway platform at one in the morning.

The street where Wilton bled and died was renamed Mayor Warren Wilton Jr. Place. The twelve cops present at his death were reassigned to Staten Island and Far Rockaway, never to be heard from again until retirement.

Henry never did tell his parents what happened. He

and his friend never spoke about it. Their diminutive heights concealed their identities among the taller people in the crowd. No one was ever charged or arrested.

Henry went to Brooklyn Technical High School and graduated at the top of his class.

He is attending MIT, pursuing a fast-track doctorate in engineering. Now and then, in his precious spare moments of reflection, he tries to calculate the odds of his fate: to kill a mayor and become an engineer. In the eyes of man and spirit, he is innocent, a blessing to his family.

CHAPTER TWENTY-THREE

What Happened to the News?

Grand Central Terminal, Manhattan, January 31, 2020

As a dog returns to its vomit, so fools repeat their folly.
Proverbs 26:11

"It's the news we're after."

Anon instructed Spin Boy and Freddie. What was going down today was big, the biggest thing they'd ever done. They had to be focused. If they lost their edge, it would bust, go all wrong, and leave them exposed. This had to be done with no slips. Anon knew they had the faith, it was there, and he was going to lead them in it, right to the end.

Everything depended on the news. She was it, though she didn't know it. She might agree if she did know it because she too had the faith. The time was ready, it was now, more than ever before, it was right, right now.

Anon, Spin Boy, and Freddie were taught when, how, and where to get it done. The time calls the person, not the other way around. The time was calling them to do it. Even if the news had all the details, she might hesitate and lose the time. The door was open to step across the threshold into a bolder place and ignite the world.

That man in Bosnia knew it a hundred and six years ago. The young man in the parking lot in Maryland did too, and he acted thirty-eight years ago. Uncle Joe took the step forward and didn't look back. Now it was their turn to move the hands of the clock closer to destiny's hour. One bold act changes the world. Destabilize the everyday order, eventually the walls come tumbling down. First them, then us. Scratch an anarchist and you always and everywhere find the cover for something entirely different.

Anon, Spin Boy, and Freddie were next in line. So was the news, even if she didn't know how next in line she would be.

Anon led them in the war against the cruel established authority that choked the life out of the oppressed. At age sixteen, he became unalterably opposed to this authority when the father of one of his classmates was killed by cops, and not just cops, but by the entire rigged, fascist system. Killed for selling singletons in front of a convenience store. The morbidly obese man struggled with the cops and suffered a fatal asthma attack. Although the system eventually paid his classmate's family several hundred thousand dollars in settlement, that served to embitter Anon more, as if money could replace an innocent life or a father's love. From then forward, Anon would strangle the life out of the cops and their masters.

Spin Boy and Freddie were shiftless potheads whom Anon found in his circle of friends. Both of them were headed nowhere in a maelstrom of unjust laws and social inequality that neither young man could cope with or understand. Anon gave them answers and direction. He made them meaningful in a place and time that previously lacked meaning for them. With Anon, they had purpose. They were agents of the Peoples' Justice Collective, and they were believers. Anon challenged them, "What are you willing to do to get it?" He also kept them well supplied with quality pot.

Anon was backed by a labyrinthine network of organizations and unnamed groups (who met in secret in their cramped apartments, with doors and windows closed, like the early church), possessing prodigious resources (one backer gave $440 million to the cause), and ties to many well-known legitimate political and nongovernmental sects. Among themselves, they referred to their network as Sila, the Polish word for "the Force." Through these linkages, Anon, Spin Boy, and Freddie, and hundreds like them, were coddled, encouraged, and fed: they were descendants of a minor but loud human aberration who, replacing reason with hate-filled emotion, centuries ago stormed the Bastille to free four forgers, a lunatic, a recaptured failed assassin from decades earlier, and a pornographer, and they called it a revolution. The revolutionaries always had the tools.

Anon's tool for today was like Anon himself – slender, dedicated, cold, hard, and lethal.

They packed their signs and took the subway to the appointed place.

Seventy-five loud, angry, resistant people can appear to be seventy-five hundred, in the right circumstances. In an enclosed space, loud passionate demonstrators overfilled their setting, pushing back at civilians and cops in an intimidating show of force. *A people united can never be divided. No justice, no peace. Advocate, demolish, destroy.*

These were more than words. This was faith, the true faith that was unconditional and total in its belief.

The Peoples' Justice Collective demands jobs, education, and health care as absolute rights for which no one should be forced to pay. We are the peoples' revolution. We fight racist police terror, sexism, LGBTQ, and ableist oppression. Abolish the police, abolish all prisons, dismantle the prison industrial complex.

The PJC was storming Grand Central Terminal. Every white person, every heterosexual, every breeder, every male is a criminal to be pushed back, resisted, exposed, and beaten, and if necessary, destroyed. History must march ahead, inexhaustibly. The collective would write the final story.

Seventy-five true believers swelled to fill the compact lower level of the terminal. Most carried signs and all were shouting. White people were cursed, and especially cops. *Cops and prisons are attacks against humanity. Paying for transportation is enslavement. Cops are the tools of slave masters. Subway fare beating is a right, not a crime. Who do you serve? Who do you protect?*

They were firm in their faith about this because so many justice warriors were their allies. The mayor and his wife, the two senators from New England, the leaders of the state legislatures. The public schools chancellor. The state's attorney general. The city council. The leadership of the party in their corner.

Anon and Freddie gave their signs to other members of the collective. "Kill the Cops." "Empty the Racist Prisons." "Fake Reforms Are Meaningless." The signs were interchangeable with each protest. One hundred and thirty-six years ago, the banners read "Poverty Is a Crime,"

"Exploitation Is Legalized Theft," and "Government Is for Slaves – Free Men Govern Themselves." The revolution was the same.

Spin Boy held his sign and kept repeating, "End racist capitalism now!" His voice, filled with righteous hatred, was the loudest of all. It echoed perfectly in the underground room, piercing ears, drawing extra attention from the confused cops.

The news was in the center of it. Her makeup was right for the occasion, although she still didn't know how fitting she looked. Her bold black eyebrows were accentuated by her animated face and toothy smile. She smiled, and though she did not chant slogans, she captured the looks of passersby, who were familiar with her due to her constant appearances on TV and social media and in print. She was a star, the movement's most youthful, outstanding star. The face of the squad. A noteworthy face. A magnet for stargazers and hero worshippers. The current lodestone of the movement. The head of the squad. Her party's vanguard.

Spin Boy consulted his watch. The takeover of Grand Central was ten minutes old. He suddenly threw his sign to the floor in exaggerated fury, sure to pull all eyes and ears to him, and let out a bloodcurdling scream, "Get your hand out of my pocket! Fascist! Get out of my pocket! Racist pig!"

His scream drained the place of all noise for a precious, strategic moment. His scene drew all eyes.

Anon was standing next to the news, with Freddie off to his left side. In a choreographed and well-rehearsed pas de deux, Anon slid his stiletto into the stomach of the news gracefully, three times. Freddie knocked down a man standing next to him, who tumbled to the floor, with Freddie yelling, "Thief! Thief!" while Anon slipped into and mingled with the crowd.

The news slumped to the floor. Her life pouring out of her, pints of blood soaking her expensive designer pants suit, the shiny green fabric turning purple as she bled to death. The expected and desired aftereffects ensued. The news media representatives beat the cops to the lump of flesh extinguishing on the floor. While attention spun to that vignette, Spin Boy, for that was how he earned his nickname, walked to the back and out of the building. His part was also rehearsed and acted flawlessly. His expertise served him well, though this was his first, and last, crucial role in the propaganda of the deed, an ages-old concept drilled into him and Freddie by Anon. The rules of engagement were fitted for terrorism.

No one would suspect the movement of killing one of its own leaders. The people behind the movement calculated that it is most effective to retell the story, after producing it. They had the public's attention in the palm of their hand. Staging the end of the news was required to implant the approved message.

She was the news because she made the news. Her sacrifice was more important than her continued value in the revolution, and if she had been able to see the whole scene, she would have accepted her part, designer pants suit and all. The faith continued to live by her death.

Having witnessed the reality, commuters from Grand Central, upon boarding their trains home, watched video of the events they had seen live minutes before, this time on their personal devices. It was, however, the video that stuck in their minds as what actually happened. They didn't trust their memories, but that video had to be the truth. It was broadcast, the proof of its veracity. The video, of course, was accompanied by commentary from per-formers, who called themselves reporters, and resident experts who explained what was being shown. This was neatly bracketed by commercials for toilet paper and beer. Arriving at home, these commuters told their families what they had witnessed; not what they had seen live, but what they had watched and heard others explain. The news is not words, noise, or thoughts. It is scripted images, repeated over and over, until it becomes the truth, expertly stage-managed.

The prompted sympathy conveyed by the media's point of view was broadcast throughout the land. That then became the facts. A sizeable segment of the public, when shown the behind-the-news manipulation, still believed it without doubt. Given the reality, they instead preferred being spoon-fed predigested pablum.

The collected public interest was not on the killer, but as planned, it was on the police. How could they let this happen, the killing of this innocent warrior, this champion of the oppressed and underpaid, this blameless woman? Surely, her racist, sexist, money-grubbing foes had snuffed her. Probably the cops were in on it. She was eulogized, and the politicians who weren't on the protest-ors' side were castigated. For Anon and his pals, this was the icing on the cake. More properly, this was the result expected by their actions. Her party's tears overflowed.

The funeral was a vulgar political rally, like every other such funeral had been previously. The city's chief dema-gogue and rabble-rouser presided. In his theatrical voice he declared, "They killed our sister, but our enemies didn't kill her spirit." The elect in attendance nodded their heads in enthusiastic assent. Coincidently, the news left this life owing thousands of dollars in deliberately unpaid taxes, like her eulogizer. Taxes were for everybody else, not the political warriors who spent, not paid, taxes.

Cut down in the prime of her mission, the news took on a new existence after death. How seamlessly the useful idiots and handmaidens, the fellow travelers and parlor believers, the overweight oppressed, the intellectually superior, and the power greedy leapt on the corpse and defiled it for good measure and reward. The corpse didn't move while it was being serviced: much the same as when she was alive.

Highlights of the funeral performances were broadcast, almost in real time, across the nation, and photographs, with written observations by writers who called themselves journalists, were published in all major newspapers and magazines. This was the reliable story of that event and the facts upon which people based their perceptions and subsequent retelling of what happened. The story was set in stone.

Soon, people who called themselves educators and academics, and were paid commensurately, began teaching about this event so that thousands of students would know the rock-solid truth, otherwise called history. The history was repeated in schools, colleges, homes, offices, and everywhere people gathered. The public was outraged. The news became gospel. Her death was venerated. The martyr was raised on a pedestal. By this light, the enemy was exposed and hounded.

Anon and his pals didn't have much time to celebrate their deed. One week after the funeral, Anon, whose given name was Jude Issacs, died of injuries inflicted on him during a break-in robbery of his Lower East Side apartment. Nothing was stolen. On the floor, next to his body, were three crisp ten-dollar bills. In his last moment here, he felt remorse, but not repentance. Later, Spin Boy committed a convenient suicide, shooting himself on the edge of a highway out of town, using his right hand, although he was left-handed. There was no vehicle found near the body. A month after, Freddie was found dead on the tracks of the Long Island Railroad, in a town he had not visited before and where he had no connections. These unfortunate occurrences were overlooked by the mainstream media and scantly reported by neighborhood papers and local news broadcasts. The separate incidents were never linked. Three moles on the posterior of humankind, gone and forgotten.

A small group of other people in the movement aware of the three, what they had done, how they died, and by whose hand, barely spoke about them and their deaths. Unlike the news, Anon, Spin Boy, and Freddie were bit players, cannon fodder really.

Soon, members of the network were summoned to Minneapolis, and other cities, to incite violence, burn stores owned by the very black people they were supposedly championing, and further the death of the system and the Man. Indeed, evil does travel far faster than love, especially when on call in chartered buses, stocked pallets of bricks ($200 per cube of five hundred, wholesale), and boxes of baseball bats at the ready, to participate in intricately planned and well-financed spontaneous riots.

In a fitting contradiction, the rioters topple statues of Lincoln, a Republican who lost his life warring against the slave states, killed by a Confederate Democrat who was first venerated by the Democrat approved and protected Ku Klux Klan, a domestic terrorist organization. In its 1920s reincarnation, the Klan was the official Democrat party of Indiana, Mississippi, Georgia, Alabama, Florida, and other states. To be elected in those states, Klan membership was the winning advantage. In a similar paradox, the rioters never touched a Planned Parenthood clinic, though its founder detested black people (she called them "weeds") as inferiors and called for their elimination by abortion, for which she received an ovation from the women's auxiliary of the Klan. Her co-founder of the abortion movement was a white supremacist Nazi-lover. He wrote that blacks were less than dirt.

What these extremists and their reign of terror have going in their favor is the intentionally cultivated lack of intelligence of vast numbers of citizens. The education monopoly plays its part in hopelessly dumbing down young people especially, and rendering them into empty vessels for the party script. The National Socialists had done all these things before, like the Reichstag fire red herring, the banning and burning of disapproved books, the nationalization of Big Brother–imposed public education curricula, and the Kristallnacht rioting and looting. Mao's Cultural Revolution utilized the same tactics, enlisting society's worst to intimidate the citizenry. Pol Pot would feel comfortable in their midst; he also defunded the police. The Acts of the Apostles tells of exactly the same recruitment of the criminal element to foment terror on the populace.

It's best when you prepare the crisis, light the fire, and then exploit it. The flyer at the January 2020 storming of

Grand Central prominently featured the calls to defund the police and abolish all prisons, two themes central to the rioting several months later, fitting like fingers in a glove. A previous US president's top adviser remarked with intended menace, "Never let a crisis go to waste." He and the president were also, deep down, Marxists.

Since the leopard can't change its spots, the current rioters readily adopt a blatantly anti-Christian, anti-Semitic rote. They deface statues of Christ and engage in an orgy of vandalizing churches. They shout their version of the blood libel lustily, holding their banners high, "Israel Kills Children." The history is available for those who look. It's not the news, though.

These rioters take advice and justification from their dead comrades in arms:

The killing of a tyrant, of an enemy of the People, is in no way to be considered as the taking of a life. To remove a tyrant is an act of liberation, the giving of life and opportunity to an oppressed people . . . Yes, the end in this case justifies the means.

The rioters follow this advice to the letter and without remorse, wishing or causing harm and death to all who disagree with their opinions. Individuality, individual thought, opinion, perspective, all to be forbidden by force. That which does not fit the approved narrative is to be canceled. Culture is what the collective says it is, as is history.

Burn. Loot. Mayhem. Skim the revolution's funds and Buy. Large. Mansions.

Uncle Joe Stalin intoned, "A single death is a tragedy, a million deaths is a statistic." Any number larger than one and any lie, no matter how vicious and false, are inconsequential in themselves for the sake of the success of the cause.

The quiet in the land must take heed.

CHAPTER TWENTY-FOUR

Alone, Alone

Lower Broadway, Manhattan, March 25, 2020

If stupidity got us into this mess, why can't it get us out?
Will Rogers

The streets were bare, as barren as waking without warning in the aftermath of a tense nightmare, and as desolate as a keening mourner at the edge of the casket, murmuring the Hail Mary through her wails.

A noiseless, empty playground jungle gym for departed children. Useless subway trains ferrying the invisible and their souls to nowhere morbidly, via a meaningless route. The lengthy, crooked street, once the passage of cows to market, where recently the prosperous shuttled between banking houses and offices, now calm and still. This was the place of fear and hiding. But it was the city. It was at once terrified of dying and afraid of living.

The city that for four hundred years had flung itself recklessly into the future was now paralyzed in limbo. Who thought the brash metropolis could be cowered so easily?

He walked. He had his camera. He hoped someday, probably not soon, he would share these photos with a few city dwellers in his circle: at this date, there was no convivial meeting of friends, except by social media. Seeing these images on a screen subdued their energy and softened their edges. Every angle in them was razor sharp, deadly to the touch. They were the record of the death of spirit and the funeral of humanity. The city was not human anymore. It was merely an extremely large, overbuilt location that was purposeless and stale. It had no smell and no taste.

The street rats were gone too. They got the word and now feasted upon their rat babies. The pigeons were clueless, per usual. They kept right on pooping on the lamp poles and the statues, unperturbed.

The city was assuredly buildings and sidewalks. That was its naked skeleton. It was drained of its blood, choked of its breath, and paralyzed in its movement. The concrete and asphalt were the final remains of triage – left to die.

It was dying, in the thrall of a slow rigor mortis, cold and ever distant to the touch, on a slab of earth and bedrock. In all its years, over generations of human habitation, it was not meant to be this. While he wept seeing it this way, his camera's eye could not cry, though it captured and held the inanimate tears. But would the city die?

Perhaps the greatest shock was coming upon places, around corners and behind trees, at intersections and in back of larger structures, that were familiar to him. His daughter played in that park after he adopted her. His first college date happened in that restaurant with the "closed until further notice" sign taped inside the door. There was the store from which he bought his morning paper and the Starbucks that supplied his first coffee of the day. He saw where the hot dog cart once stood, redolent of the acrid odor of reused greasy water. He remembered that smell with intensity.

He was in the grip of the laws of inertia. Though the city's life had ceased, his first response was life had to continue. He couldn't, for the time being, reconcile what he was seeing with what he felt and remembered. This was spirit memory, like a toned muscle suddenly gone to flab, trying to flex. The urge was there but the faculty was unresponsive.

These memories came painfully. He was overcome with the need to rest, close his eyes, and be still. On a bench at the foot of Broadway, he was alone and he sat, camera untouched by his side. The wooden seat was hard. Its position in the midday sun warmed him. Surrounded by giant buildings, in sight of the massive bulk of the Custom House (with no one camping on its steps) and close enough to the *Charging Bull* (with no one posing next to it) to see its snorting visage, he shut out the light and knelt his mind. He was on sacred ground.

The week before, he'd walked down Broadway. Stores were open and dozens of people strolled, though by the look of it they were out for a walk, not to and from work. That seemed a normal day under the circumstances – there were voices, smiles, movement; the heat of human bodies, the vibration and incense of city life.

It wasn't only the bodies that were missing, it was the spirit, the rhythm, the nerve. The tension was gone, with its constant hum of anger, joy, impatience, bitterness, and anticipation. The void was incalculable, like a built-up black hole, stagnant and empty of sensation, held up by what? Four invisible pillars? Aching emptiness. If there was a prayer for this situation, he didn't know the catechism. This had been, recently, a boisterous cathedral of the living on a solid foundation.

He opened his eyes and saw his camera by his side. He was photographing a massive yawning vacancy. This was a created wilderness. He couldn't take a picture of desire or loss or grief. The pictures themselves were not the objects caught in a second. The pictures were objects in themselves, in many aspects not representative of the things they glimpsed. An angle in any direction changed what was the end result on film. He was nostalgic for, he yearned and hungered for, an emotion. An emotion he knew before being alone. Photographs don't hold emotions; they trigger them. The city, when alive, was an emotion, his life's emotion interred in his jumbled soul.

Was this the watch, the wake, or the final rites? As a very lapsed Catholic, he nonetheless whispered silently, *Agnes Dei, qui tollis peccata mundi, dona eis requiem.* When does missing a part of life start to be so consuming that the sensation of loss eats at the heart and soul? He was staring into the box at the body that was waiting to be buried. Had anyone told the corpse it was dead? Would it be buried faintly alive, capable of reviving by a miracle or extreme human intervention? He contemplated the absolute terror of being buried in a comatose state, seeing and hearing, even feeling and smelling, but unable to register resistance, helplessly experiencing the dirt mounded on the coffin. "I surrender, but say the word and I will be healed," he pleaded out loud involuntarily.

In the end, and he hoped this wasn't the end, do we

sentence ourselves to "sing sad and bitter songs of disillusion and defeat"? Is it time for an elegy? He knew that if the city survived this, there would always be a massive, deep scar over a tender wound, and the obvious vulnerability would be an aftermath too difficult to ignore. Who wants to disturb the scab? One survives a breakdown fully aware that the vicious specter of the nemesis relapse is never distant.

This was all too awful to be harbored for any more time and effort. He stood and turned to walk back up Broadway. If he followed it uptown, past West Twenty-Third Street where he lived, into Midtown, the Upper West Side, Harlem, Fort Tryon, Inwood, the Bronx, then Yonkers and points north, maybe the complete path to Albany, like the settlers did, would there be life? Could he find it on a pilgrimage like the early Irish monks, to whom all of life was a pilgrimage? Would he progress? To where?

He vowed to try, not all at once, but in increments, day by day. What else was there to do: Accept the loss? He would not die this way, watching the gravediggers cover the coffin and the attendees remark, "It was wonderful once."

At the end of every road, you meet yourself.
S. N. Behrman, playwright

ACKNOWLEDGEMENTS

Perhaps the anecdote attributed to Picasso, after he saw the cave paintings in Lascaux, France dating from thirty-thousand years ago, is correct: "We have learned nothing." I search for answers to questions that, I suspect, are as old as human time itself.

Of the writers who inspire, William Faulkner, ramrod tall and brilliant, sits in the saddle of his favorite horse, surveying the landscape – a stirring sight. His grammar of the soul, in its many expressions, shines a bright light still, fifty-eight years after his death and the publication of his last novel. No writer can ever surmount his place, painting the human condition and the still decaying world in words. I mourn his untimely loss every time I sit down to practice, as a virgin adolescent, the craft he mastered. His quotes and paraphrases of his statements are used in the preface and chapter 20.

My first thanks are due to my Father and Redeemer and Spirit, then to Edna Lorraine Pernell Shaw, Carleton Shaw, Paul (or Paull) Santonocito (whomever and where-ever you are), LeRoy Pernell, Fred and Paula Kleinfeld, Uncle Daniel Cilenti, Steve Ma, and the rest of my family.

I am especially grateful to my wife and to my youngest son for whispering "Daddy is writing, give him some peace," countless times over two years.

Thanks to my friends at Curley's Diner for the lunchtime conversations, especially "Dark Gable" Robert and Maria Aposporos. Thanks to Nick Inglima for sharing tales of Sicily. Pieces of their stories are told here with affection and respect. Thank you, Elaine Berg, for telling me what your mother told you – I'm trying to live my life and not die a fool. Thank you Nancie Urcioli Johnson, Ricki Goe, and Barbara Susan Diorio for your memories about Italian family dining habits. A nod to the late Chickie Cotel for a particular anecdote in chapter 5.

A special thanks to David Domke, whose photographs touched me deeply at a time when other images could not. Thank you, Reverends Mark Snyder, Richard Burke and Dan Hintz, and the Scarsdale Community Baptist Church Adult Bible School, led by Darryl Smith. My thanks to Swaine Napier for sharing his insights on faith.

Credit is due to the works of Aeschylus (*The Persians,* 472 BCE), William Shakespeare (*King Lear,* 1606, *Twenty-Ninth Sonnet*, 1609, and *All's Well That Ends Well,* 1623), John Bunyan (*The Pilgrim's Progress from This World, to That Which Is to Come,* 1678), John Filson on Daniel Boone (1784), James McNeill Whistler (*The Gentle Art of Making Enemies,* 1890), O. Henry (*The Four Million,* 1906), Edith Wharton (*The Age of Innocence,* 1920), C. S. Lewis ("The Weight of Glory," 1941), Edith Hamilton (*Mythology,* 1942, quoted in the preface), Tennessee Williams (and Edwina D. Williams, *The Glass Menagerie,* 1945), John Steinbeck (Nobel address, 1962, and *Travels with Charley,* 1962), William Manchester (*The Death of a President,* 1967; and with Paul Reid, *The Last Lion,* 2012), Dr. R. D. Laing (quoted in chapter 20 from *"I've Seen Better Days,"* 1970, and in chapter 24 from *The Politics of Experience and the Bird of Paradise,* 1967), Robert Caro (*The Power Broker,* 1974, and *Working,* 2019), Peter Mayle (*Toujours Provence,*

1991), Ha Jin ("Saboteur," 1997), Helen McPhail (*The Long Silence*, 1999), Edmund Morris (*Theodore Rex*, 2001), Jay Parini (*One Matchless Time,* 2004), Dr. Thomas Sowell (*A Man of Letters*, 2007), Paul J. Hill (*Mix My Blood with the Blood of the Unborn,* 2008, quoted in chapter 23), Candice Millard (*Destiny of the Republic*, 2011), Simon Sebag Montefiore (paraphrased in chapter 18 and quoted in chapter 20 from *Jerusalem: The Biography,* 2012), Ari Shavit (*My Promised Land*, 2013), John Hooper (*The Italians*, 2015, quoted in the preface), and Scott S. Greenberger (*The Unexpected President*, 2017) for the inspiration they gave to these stories.

Luke 4:1-13 is paraphrased in chapter 7. Paul in Acts 20:24 and John 18:10 are cited in chapter 11. Luke 6:38 is paraphrased in chapter 14. Psalm 69:23 is paraphrased in chapter 18. John 9:1-41 is cited in chapter 20. Acts 19:23-40 is paraphrased in chapter 22, as is Psalm 35:20.

Art critic Lady K Flo is quoted in the preface about Paul Cèzanne.

My banker, Carol Garzillo, contributed an anecdote about her grandfather that made its way into chapter 8.

The French physiologist Claude Bernard (*Lectures on the Phenomena of Life Common to Animals and Plants,* 1974) is paraphrased in chapter 9. Rex Stout's story "Christmas Party" (1957) is quoted in chapter 9.

Sir Winston Churchill's quotes in chapter 9 are from *The Wit of Sir Winston* (1965) by Adam Sykes and Iain Sproat.

Pastor J. Amos Jones of Friendship Missionary Baptist Church is quoted in chapter 12, from his sermon (October 2, 2016). Thomas Merton is also cited in chapter 12 (*Contemplation and Compassion*, 1960).

A quote in the preface is from Dick Cavett's interview of Salvador Dalí on February 11, 1971. Material in chapter 14 is drawn from two episodes of *The Dick Cavett Show*, original broadcast dates December 16, 1985, and October 7, 1986.

Dr. Alfred Adler is cited in the preface and chapter 17 (*What Life Could Mean to You*, 1998). Erik Larson's *The Splendid and the Vile* (2020) is cited in chapter 17, quoting Sir Winston Churchill.

A quote in chapter 18, attributed by some sources to Lenin, is not to be confused with a completely different quote attributed to Helen Keller: "The only thing worse than being blind is having sight and no vision." Freud's theory of worrying strangeness ("The Uncanny," 1919) is paraphrased in chapter 18, as is a quote from Vince Lombardi.

West German politician Willy Brandt is quoted in chapter 19 from Greg Mitchell's *The Tunnels* (2016). Sigmund Freud is paraphrased in chapter 19 ("Leonardo da Vinci: A Memory of His Childhood," 1910).

Alexander Berkman (*Prison Memoirs of an Anarchist*, 1912) and Emma Goldman (*Living My Life*, 1931) are quoted in chapter 23. Dan Bongino is paraphrased there as well.

I'm grateful to Opus Dei for my study of the Way and the Work with them.

The late Reverend Sarah Eynstone, chaplain of St. Paul's Cathedral, London, is remembered for her instructive observation on the Last Supper.

Thanks to my editors, Randy Ladenheim-Gil, Heather Rodino, and Jon Ford. Jon, you know what I'm writing better than I do – every jot of your red pen educates me:

you are one of my blessings.

Although his work is not cited in this book, the late David Bohm's *On Dialogue* (1996) was an inspiration for me during my writing. A dear friend, David A. Browne, gifted me a copy of this book, and the ideas it contains have engaged me ever since.

Thanks to Martin Drew (although I knew his first name, I didn't address my junior high school teachers as anyone other than Mister or Missus), who believed a fifteen-year-old in Bedford-Stuyvesant in 1970 could understand and appreciate Chaucer, Milton, Swift, Shakespeare, and the glory of the English language. I read and absorbed, memorized and recited, and in the process fell hopelessly in love with this majesty of a tongue and its gorgeous mysteries. Wherever he is, I owe him an enormous debt I cannot repay.

Dr. David Burnham advised me, "All of life is a research project." He was correct.

A note of thanks goes to the late Dr. Thomas Flanagan, and to Harry Klaff and Robert Silverman. They instilled in me a passion for organized research and the pursuit of questions. I am in their debt.

To everyone, famous, infamous, and anonymous, the shards of whose stories may be found here, a gathering of broken mirrors, thank you.

ABOUT ATMOSPHERE PRESS

Atmosphere Press is an independent, full-service publisher for excellent books in all genres and for all audiences. Learn more about what we do at atmospherepress.com.

We encourage you to check out some of Atmosphere's latest releases, which are available at Amazon.com and via order from your local bookstore:

The Embers of Tradition, a novel by Chukwudum Okeke

Saints and Martyrs: A Novel, by Aaron Roe

When I Am Ashes, a novel by Amber Rose

Melancholy Vision: A Revolution Series Novel, by L.C. Hamilton

The Recoleta Stories, by Bryon Esmond Butler

Voodoo Hideaway, a novel by Vance Cariaga

Hart Street and Main, a novel by Tabitha Sprunger

The Weed Lady, a novel by Shea R. Embry

A Book of Life, a novel by David Ellis

It Was Called a Home, a novel by Brian Nisun

Grace, a novel by Nancy Allen

Shifted, a novel by KristaLyn A. Vetovich

Because the Sky is a Thousand Soft Hurts, stories by Elizabeth Kirschner

ABOUT THE AUTHOR

Anthony E. Shaw is a management consultant, former chief examiner and deputy mayor of the City of Yonkers, New York, and founder and former director of the Internal Control Unit of the New York City Department of Investigation. He served as North American vice president for human resources at Danzas/AEI Air and Ocean Logistics. He is a proud product of Bedford-Stuyvesant, Brooklyn, and a graduate of New York City public schools and City University. He is the author of *The Faithful Manager* (2013) and *Wolfe Studies* (2020). He lives in Scarsdale, New York, with his wife, Bonnie, who is a proud American of Chinese descent, and son, Ethan, a bilingual American of Chinese-Sicilian-African American descent.